Permanent Resident
at the Altar

Permanent Resident at the Altar

Keisha Bass

URBAN
CHRISTIAN

Urban Books, LLC
97 N18th Street
Wyandanch, NY 11798

ISBN 13: 978-1-62286-813-1
ISBN 10: 1-62286-813-7

First Trade Paperback Printing November 2015
Printed in the United States of America

10 9 8 7 6 5 4 3 2 1

Distributed by Kensington Publishing Corp.
Submit Orders to:
Customer Service
400 Hahn Road
Westminster, MD 21157-4627
Phone: 1-800-733-3000
Fax: 1-800-659-2436

Permanent Resident at the Altar

by

Keisha Bass

To all the single ladies, waiting, desiring, and praying for the man you will join in holy matrimony.

May God bless you and keep you, as you put your trust in Him and His timing.

For we walk by faith, not by sight.

—II Corinthians 5:7

Chapter One

It had been a year since Ava had given it all to God for guidance through her life. He had led her into accepting what she could not change and forgiveness for herself and others. She glanced at Kevin, her boyfriend, and thought back to all she had been through.

How could she have been so easily turned to the enemy? Ava's one mistake led her into a tailspin of lows. The impulsive behavior caused her to almost lose her best friend forever. As much as she wanted to blame the entire incident on the alcohol she had consumed, she couldn't. Sleeping with her best friend's fiancé was only the start of stepping down the hill onto the path of transgression and ultimate betrayal.

When she received news of her pregnancy, a result of her undeniable mistake, her life turned into pure devastation, and she felt unwilling to go on. Her closest friend pushed her into getting the help she needed. The CCC became her refuge in her time of turmoil and uncertainty. After a few months of therapy and group sessions with prayer, she finally learned to forgive herself and let God handle her mayhem within, including her self-esteem, something she had struggled with most of her life.

Putting God into her life, to let Him lead her where she needed to be, gave her great pride. She had her biggest believer on her side, and she had confidence that He would only lead her in the right direction. Because she let God lead, she was blessed with the man she imagined having for the rest of her life. *God is good, all the time; All the time, God is good.*

Butterflies break danced in Ava's stomach as she and Kevin traveled, fingers intertwined, to his mother's house. Looking forward to meeting the woman she hoped would one day be her mother-in-law depleted her emotional bank account. Only withdrawals were made and nothing was deposited. Excitement, nervousness, hope, and apprehension all flooded out of her heart.

Three months before, their first official date occurred at her girlfriend Toni's vow renewal ceremony. Ava and Kevin danced the night away, and had spent almost every day together since that evening. Things between them blossomed perfectly according to Ava's schedule, and now she was headed to meet Gladys, Kevin's mother, for the first time.

What would his mother think of her? How much did Kevin tell her about how they met at the Christian Counseling Center under very unfavorable circumstances? Did she know what had happened to Ava? Did Kevin let her in on everything? Did Ava wear the right outfit that exuded a humble confidence and said, "I'm the perfect woman for your son"?

Glancing at Kevin's handsome, chiseled profile calmed Ava's anxieties. He had proved to be the real deal, what her heart needed and had been waiting for all her adult life. God had brought them together, and what God put together, no man or woman, even a mother, could pull apart. *Right?*

So why was Ava so uneasy? Why did she feel the need to have Kevin stop the car and head in the opposite direction? He would surely be mad.

Her thoughts were interrupted by her cell phone vibrating through her purse. She located the phone and read the text message.

"Who's that, babe?" Kevin's concern made her feel special.

"Just my mother. She's reminding me about my cousin's wedding next Saturday." Ava tossed the phone back in her handbag. "Like I'd forget I'm a bridesmaid. Why wouldn't I show up? I didn't buy the hideous dress for no reason."

"Oh, yeah." He chuckled. "I almost forgot."

"You did?"

"No, I'm just joking. I can't wait to get all beautified up with you and have a nice time."

"I don't know how much of a nice time we'll have. My mother and aunt aren't that close, so my cousin and I aren't either. I think I was chosen because I was one of only two girl cousins in the family."

Kevin soothingly caressed her hand. "Well, at any rate, you and I will have a good time gettin' our dance on and our eat on. We'll just focus on that. Deal?"

"Deal." Ava loved how he could always look on the positive side of situations. She needed that in her life, and she needed him in her life. Hopefully, his mother would see it that way too. Her nerves bubbled over. Ava should've taken a shot of something before Kevin picked her up, but it was too late now. Ms. Gladys would get 100 percent her. Hopefully, that would be good enough.

"You okay, Ava?"

She giggled. "Why, is my unusual silence a giveaway?"

"You just seem deep in thought."

"I'm sorry." She rubbed her hands together. "Just a bit nervous."

"You don't have to be sorry. Or nervous." He grinned. "My mom will love you."

"Did you tell her how we met?"

Clearing his throat, he moved his hand and held the steering wheel firmly with both hands. "Well, she did ask. And I've never lied to my mother a day in my life."

Her head dropped.

"But that shouldn't matter. She loves me, and I love you, so that's all that matters."

Ava was sure her smile could be seen from down the street. "You love me?" This was the first time she'd heard those words flow out of his mouth. They sounded beautiful.

"I sure do."

"I love you too, Kevin." The red light provided the perfect time for the couple to meet in the middle for a passionate lip lock. Her heart danced. "I think that's why I'm so nervous. I really want her to like me."

"Just be you and she will."

There were his sweet, simple, comforting words. God had answered every one of her prayers concerning a man. Kevin's personality filled the gaps in her life where she struggled. They were good for one another, and now, as he confessed his love for her, the day was perfect. Nothing could erase the smile on her face.

After pulling into the driveway, Kevin hopped out of the car and hustled to Ava's side of the car. He opened the door for her and then took Ava's hand as they walked through the front door of his mother's house. She was hoping to transfer her nerves by touch to him so she could act like herself.

He looked left and right into the rooms decorated in contemporary décor. "Momma, we're here."

"I'm in the kitchen, baby."

A stout, poised woman with full locks sauntered her way into the room with open arms. In her smile, Ava could see Kevin's handsome face. As he embraced his mother, the love between them was evident.

"Momma, this is Ava." He presented her as a proud child would show off his show-and-tell toy to his class.

Ava stuck out her hand. "Nice to meet you, Ms. Allen."

His mother's hand, rigid and unwelcoming, barely grabbed hold of Ava's. "Nice to meet you." She examined Ava up and down, judgmental glare included.

Ava's nerves shot throughout her body. *Don't say the wrong thing. What's the right thing? Lord, please help.*

"So, Momma, what have you been up to since I saw you last?" Kevin gently kissed his mother's cheek.

"Same ol', same ol'." She patted his back as he squeezed her tight. "Not much has changed except the doctor upped my blood pressure medicine."

"Why'd he do that?"

"He says I need to relax more, but I don't do nothing."

Kevin rubbed his forehead. "When's the last time Tweet was by here?"

Ava knew that Tweet, Kevin's baby sister, was the main reason for a lot of the family's stress. He never went into details, but she knew there was something more to it than a little sister hanging with the wrong crowd. All Ava could do was to keep her in prayer.

"I don't know . . . about a week ago." His mom placed a casserole dish on the middle of the dining table. "I called her to invite her over for dinner tonight, but no answer. So I sent her a text."

Kevin looked conflicted about what words would come out of his mouth next. "Well, Momma, you know she only comes around when she needs something. You don't need to worry yourself about that. Let me worry for you. That's what the doctor is talking about. Try to relax. I'll take care of Tweet."

"I know, baby, but you have enough going on." His mother fidgeted with the place settings. "I'll just keep sending up my prayers and try not to worry so much, but I can't help but think of all the danger she could be into out there running those streets."

Ava walked toward the kitchen where Kevin and his mother now stood. "Is there anything I can do? Pray? I can put her on the prayer list at church."

His mother put her hand on her hip. "That's sweet, Ava, but this is a family matter, and you're not family."

Okay, won't offer ever again. Ava turned her head away from his mother and pursed her lips.

"Momma, don't be ridiculous. Ava doesn't have to be family to pray for Tweet." Kevin strolled over to Ava and reached for her hand and squeezed it tight. "Besides, she may be family one day, and you know Tweet could use all the prayers she can get."

Ms. Allen, seeming ashamed of her response, smiled. "Of course. I apologize, Ava. Just not myself lately." She touched Kevin's shoulder as she passed by him. "I'll be right back."

Waiting until she was out of sight, Ava gritted her teeth. "Your mother doesn't seem to care for me too much."

"Don't worry, babe." He put his arms around her waist. "She is just so stressed out. I can tell."

Ava melted into his warm embrace. "I feel helpless not able to do anything, but I will continue to keep her in my prayers."

Kevin stepped back and rubbed his massive hand over Ava's back. "I appreciate you, but Tweet is a whole other story. I know you are familiar with bits and pieces of her story, but she has created enough havoc for a lifetime. Right now, we're not sure where she's living or who she's with."

Ava leaned in for a hug. "How old is she?"

"She'll be twenty-five this spring."

"Well, I know you care for her, but she is a grown woman. You all shouldn't put that much pressure on yourselves. She's gonna do what she wants to do whether you say anything to her or not."

Kevin walked over to the dinner table and slid into a seat. "But you don't understand. She's my only little sister."

Ava followed, taking the seat next to his and placing her hand on his leg. "Well, help me to understand."

He took a deep breath. "All right, here goes." Kevin hesitated.

Putting her hand under his chin, Ava turned his head and looked straight into his eyes. "You know you can tell me anything, right?"

"Yeah, I know." He took hold of her hand and rubbed it in his hands. "When I was in college and she was a freshman in high school, I thought it was funny to let her smoke weed every once in a while with me and my buddies." He threw his hands up. "I know; I'm a terrible big brother."

Ava squeezed his hands. "You're not a terrible brother or person. Things happen. Everyone makes mistakes. You were young."

"And stupid." He scoffed. "And the worst part is when I started dabbling in cocaine, Tweet followed suit."

"Mmm. So you feel like it's your fault?"

"Of course I do. But she didn't stop there. She moved on to meth, has done Ecstasy here and there, and will do just about anything she can get her hands on now. A friend of mine told me he saw her with what looked to be some crackheads hanging downtown."

"That's enough of telling your sister's business." His mother rushed out of the kitchen. "If Ava wants to pray, that's fine, but she doesn't need to know all the details. Like I said, this is a family matter." His mother peered into Ava's eyes.

Ava surrendered her hands in the air. "No problem. I don't want it to be an issue. Just talking to Kevin about what's bothering him. Seeing as he listens to everyone else's problems at the center, I'm just trying to be here for him. Not looking to cause any trouble, ma'am."

"Yeah, Momma, we were just talking."

"Well, find something else to talk about." She picked up the casserole from the table and headed back toward the kitchen. "In fact, y'all can let yourselves out. I don't feel much like eating anymore."

"We're not gonna have dinner, Momma?" Kevin stood and walked over to his mother.

"You can have it all you want, but I'm going to my room. Eat. Don't eat. Doesn't matter to me." She sulked as she headed out of the room. "I'm going to lie down. Nice to have met you, Ava."

"You too, Ms. Allen." *Not.*

"I've never seen her like this. Maybe I should go talk to her."

"Do what you need to do, Kevin. I'll be here"—Ava folded her arms—"waiting."

His forehead wrinkled in despair. "I'll just come back and check on her later. Let's go to our favorite restaurant."

Ava breathed a sigh of relief. She didn't want to stay there a minute longer. One big question that loomed in her mind was how could Kevin, so sweet and a man of impeccable character, ever come out of the womb of that woman? Stressed out or not, she didn't have to treat Ava that way, or be so rude to the woman her son was in love with.

Sure, his mother knew that Ava and Kevin met under less-than-favorable circumstances, but God had done a miracle in Ava's life as He continued to move her forward in her walk with Him in a positive manner. Didn't that count for anything? *Ms. Allen could at least take time to get to know the woman in her son's life before passing any judgments.*

Ava was definitely falling for Kevin. In fact, she had fallen and hadn't been able to get up. Kevin was it for her, the man she had been waiting for all of her life, but this gigantic red flag with Kevin's mother's face as the symbolic crest aggravated everything she felt for him. Would they be able to move forward, or should Ava move on? Was this the sign she shouldn't ignore?

Not ever being one to back down from a challenge, Ava tossed thoughts around that this particular situation might prove to involve a little more than she was willing to deal with. She pictured herself more than once walking down the aisle to Kevin, but not one time did she imagine the mother of the groom sitting in the front row wearing a look of disapproval on her face. A great relationship with her future mother-in-law and someone who approved of her and wore a smile on her son's wedding day was what Ava had always had in her visions of the life-changing day.

Ava would have to do some rethinking along with a great deal of prayer. She wanted to be married more than anything, but after the ring was finally on her finger, she didn't want to live in hell trying to please her mother-in-law and fight for her husband's attention. Her dream never included a struggle of that proportion. Maybe she needed to rethink the dream in its entirety, or reconsider the object of her dream, no matter how sweet or handsome he was. Either way, something would need to change, and his mother's attitude was at the top of Ava's list.

Chapter Two

I really like Kevin, but—

"Ava!" Rene clapped her hands.

How long had Ava tuned out whatever Rene was talking about? "Yes."

Rene's head tilted like a mother scolding her young child. "Where are you, girl? I've been talking to you for the past five minutes."

"I'm sorry, girl." She giggled. "Just mulling stuff over in my head. What were you saying?"

"Nothing much, just I appreciate you meeting me here. This is one of two places I've narrowed it down to for the new law office of Rene Jacobs, attorney-at-law." She took a curtsy. "Doesn't that sound nice?"

"Yes, it does, Ms. Attorney-at-law. I want you to know how proud of you I am. You are stepping out on faith and acting on what the Lord has put in your heart." Ava gazed out of the front window. "I hope to do the same one day. Catering is a nice side gig, but one day soon I want to leave the probation officer thing and open my own restaurant."

"And I believe you'll do it, Ava. You just got to believe in you."

"I'm trying." She waved her hand in the air.

"Yep, all your dreams are coming true. You are healthier and happier these days, working on your restaurant goals, and let's not forget that handsome man of God who

I'm sure one day you'll call your husband." Rene beamed as if making an official announcement.

"Not so sure about that last one." Ava had hoped many times over that that would be her and Kevin's outcome, but she didn't need her or any of her friends getting ahead of themselves.

"Why? What's up with you and Kevin?"

"Nothing's wrong with us." Ava leaned over the arm of the mocha-colored couch, hoping that once she told Rene what happened, her friend would tell her she was looking at it all wrong. "But I did meet his mother the other night and, I gotta say, it didn't go so well."

"Really? What happened?" Her friend's concern was sweet.

"Not sure, really. First, she gave one of those stank shakes. You know, like she really didn't want to touch my hand."

Rene shook her head. "I know exactly what you mean. I hate those."

"I know, right? Anyway, all I did was express an interest in his baby sister, Tweet, and her drug issues. I offered to pray for her and her situation, or at least put her on the prayer list at church." Ava placed her hand on her hip, proud that after she had shed forty pounds, she found a hip to put her hand on. "And do you know his mother counteracted with an attitude?"

"Maybe you misunderstood her." Rene picked up a plastic flower arrangement sprinkled with pink and purple petals.

"Don't think so. She actually said I didn't have to pray for her because it was a family matter."

"Are you serious?" Rene sat back in the desk chair. "And what did Kevin have to say?"

"He just chalked it up to her being stressed out and worried about Tweet."

Ava hadn't decided yet if Kevin had chosen sides. She didn't want to come between a man and his mother, but she didn't want to be treated like a sucka either. Remaining optimistic would be difficult, but she could do it. The next time she and his mother came together, hopefully the result would turn out in a more favorable, positive manner. She wanted to believe that anyway. Ava would have to pray on it.

"Maybe that was the case and next time it will be different." Rene's eyes softened as she lifted her eyebrows.

Her girlfriend's comment confirmed her thoughts. Ava was now ready to turn her focus to something else. "So does the other spot have these big, beautiful windows with a view of the park?" She lifted her hands toward the windows to present the view to Rene.

"No, it doesn't. And this is a bigger space as well. Room for growth." Rene had gone from lawyer to Realtor in less than five seconds.

"I really like it. I know I haven't laid eyes on the other place, but this just seems like you. I could see you here, Rene, helping people and getting justice for those who can't get it for themselves."

Rene jumped out of her chair, smiling. "I was hoping you'd say that. I have a confession."

"Okay." Ava froze and braced herself for what she was sure would be exciting news.

"I put a deposit down on this place. I was counting on you liking it." She welcomed Ava into an embrace.

Ava needed that hug for more than a few reasons. Although she had started talking about another topic, the issue with Kevin's mother wasn't far from her mind. "And what if I didn't like it?"

"Then I would've taken you to the other spot. I haven't signed any contracts yet, but I'm glad you're on board with this place. Now I can start putting things in motion."

She searched through her phone. "He said I could move in as early as next week."

"Great. And I can help you with that, too. Just give me a few days' heads-up so I can clear my schedule."

"I was hoping your bighead brother would be available too, as we'll need some manpower to move some furniture."

"I'll ask him. I'm sure it's not a problem."

"Awesome." Rene smiled. "Is this really happening?"

"Did you ever think otherwise?" Ava always knew Rene would have her own practice one day. She exuded confidence in her profession, and a lot of times, that's half the battle.

Scanning the room as if she needed to take it all in, Rene said, "Nope, not really, but I just can't believe this day is really here."

"I'm happy for you, lady." Ava opened her arms for a hug. "You deserve it."

"I do, don't I?" Rene giggled at her comment as she leaned into the tight squeeze.

"Yes, so enjoy it."

After all Rene had been through, and all that Ava had helped to usher her into the last year or so, she deserved to have her dreams come true. Rene, special inside and out, lived with a humble spirit that surely paved the way for the Lord's favor to go before her and shower her with all she had hoped for and deserved. Life's road wasn't always smooth, but Rene was a great example of allowing God to avenge the wrongs done in her life. He had come through in her life.

Ava had come out stronger on the other side of her storms and deserved to have her dreams come true too. She believed God would bless her with her dreams as well, so she would follow Rene's lead and step out on faith. Their avenues may have been a little different, but their goals were the same: true fulfillment and authentic happiness.

For Ava, her obstacles weren't property deeds, advertising, or trying to build a client list. No, her obstacle had birthed the current love in her life; the man she pictured the rest of her life with; her best friend, partner in crime, and the father of her children one day.

His mother seemed to have a certain place in his life, which was perfectly fine. A man only treats his significant other as well as he treats his mother. Ava just hoped there was enough room in his life for her. Her heart had already put an emotional deposit down on Kevin and their future together; hopefully his mother wouldn't hold the contract for ransom.

Chapter Three

Three days later, Ava found herself standing at the church altar wearing a counterfeit smile and a hideous pink dress that transformed her into a bottle of Pep-to-Bismol. The atmosphere and décor were lovely, but Ava picked apart the things she would do differently on her special day. She knew the colors, the florist she would use, and where the reception would be held. All she had to do to choose her favorite wedding dress was visit her Pinterest page. The only missing piece of the puzzle was the right man to stand beside her on that holy day of matrimony.

Kevin grinned at her handsomely from the audience as he stood with the rest of the guests while her cousin, Melonie, floated down the aisle to her groom.

Although they had spent time together the past few days, she and Kevin avoided the conversation they needed to have about his mother. All Ava got out of him was that Tweet had shown up to his mom's house and slept for two days. Glad to know his sister was all right, she enjoyed the positive news and figured they could revisit the negative issues at a later date.

How did she get scammed into standing up for her cousin? She hadn't really talked to Melonie since they were in college, and before that since they were kids. It was a nice excuse for her and Kevin to get all dolled up and have a night out besides their usual dinner or coffee, though, and for the first time in a long time, her mother wouldn't be able to ask why she didn't have a date. Her mother would be satisfied, and that meant Ava would be satisfied too.

Ava's mother loved Kevin and the fact that he had come into her life. Even though the circumstances weren't great, the result was an encouraging move forward for them all. Two of the most important people in her life seemed to cherish their relationship as much as they cherished Ava. She only wished her relationship with his mother would resemble at least half of what they shared.

As the service continued, Ava inserted herself and her husband-to-be every step of the way. She didn't hear the bride's or groom's vows. The words she would say and words she hoped to hear one day rang louder in her mind than the conversation at hand.

When the new husband and wife walked back down the aisle hand in hand, Ava came out of her daydream of casting herself as the lead role in the wedding ceremony. Guests followed the couple and the wedding party then filed into the adjoining room that displayed a glossy wooden dance floor, DJ booth, and an open bar. The fuchsia glass candle centerpieces on each table for eight set a soothing atmosphere. As the couple found their table up front with the rest of the wedding party, Ava hoped the atmosphere would stay that way: soothing and peaceful.

By the time the entrées arrived, Kevin had sipped the last of his sweet tea. "Man, I'm glad the food is here. I am too hungry."

"Mmm, usually I'm the first to say that." She giggled.

He bent his head as he pressed his warm finger against her lips. "Uh-uh. I told you about that, Ava. Making jokes like that is negative to your self-image, and I'm not having it. If you're hungry, you can say you're hungry. God put food on this earth for a reason."

Ava batted her eyelashes. "Thank you, hon, but you know old habits die hard."

"I know, but talking about yourself in that manner doesn't add to your life one bit. I won't have you putting yourself down, Miss Alexander. You got that?"

"Yes, Mr. Allen." She kissed him on the cheek. Ava wasn't sure if she was more attracted to him in these moments, when his overwhelming protectiveness from everything potentially harmful to Ava's self-esteem, including her own hurtful comments, would take center stage. This was tied with watching him raise his hands high in the air in church during worship. Seeing a man's sincere worship of his Creator was a trait that was beyond attractive. Good thing Ava didn't have to choose, because there were so many things she had fallen in love with. These two were just at the top of the list.

Sauntering up with open arms, Ava's parents' smiles grew bright as they saw their daughter. Ava suspected they had different reasons. Her father was happy to see her; her mother was happy to see her with a man.

Ava stood and threw her arms out wide. "Hi, Momma and Daddy."

"Hey, baby." Her father grinned as he welcomed his daughter into his arms. "Good to see you. Y'all having a good time?"

"Sure am, Daddy. This is nice. Just about to eat. Y'all got here just in time."

"Yes, sir, Mr. Alexander. Even though Ava says she plans to outshine me on the dance floor, I told her we'll just have to see about that."

They all chuckled. Kevin resembled a small child tattling. Ava adored his childlike qualities. He kept her laughing and kept her young.

"Now don't let her fool you, Kevin." Her father speaking to the love of her life was endearing and caressed Ava's heart with warm feelings of comfort. She hoped the two men in her life and their conversations would grow in their relationship and be the norm as they transformed into a family one day. "I'm the one who taught her those moves, so she can't take credit for nothing she shows you."

Her mother rolled her eyes.

"Yes, Daddy, you did." Ava sighed. "I got it all from you."

"What? I'm just telling the truth." Her dad did his best dance moves, popping his shoulders and bouncing his head. "Look at that. Ooh, I better stop before y'all try to steal my moves."

"Ain't nobody stealing your moves, Daddy. And yes, I know. You are the bomb dancer. You remind us every time we talk about dancing."

"Yeah, honey." Ava's mother patted his hand. "You'll have your chance to show off, dear. One day when Ava has her wedding, you two can do a dance-off."

Ava shot a glance at her mother, as she knew one of her mother's comments was due to arrive sooner rather than later. She possessed a talent for always finding one way or another to throw Ava's potential wedding day or marriage into the conversation whenever Kevin was around. She just couldn't help herself. Ava preferred that she did help herself, but she had already briefed Kevin on her mother's pushy demeanor that showed up more often than not. Embarrassing? Yes. Annoying? Yes. But it wasn't anything she, or Kevin, couldn't handle.

"Yes, Momma. Daddy and I will be able to get our groove on competition-style one day at my reception when I get married. Got it."

"I know you don't like for me to say it, but I know you'll have your day." Her mother shot a glance and a smile toward Kevin. "One day soon, perhaps?"

"Moth-er." Ava tilted her head. "Enough already."

"She's fine, Ava." Kevin waved his hand in the air. "In fact, I don't mind it at all. What mother or father wouldn't hope that their child's relationship is a good one and headed toward marriage? But one thing's for sure, Mrs. Alexander: what I try to live by is that when God's timing is right, mine will be too."

"Ooh, Ava. What a wonderful way to put it, Kevin. And you can call me Lydia." Her mother patted him on the shoulder. "And I guess I'll just be quiet then. But, Ava"—she looked at Ava and winked—"he's a keeper."

He definitely was a keeper. If he could get her mother to shut her mouth like that, Kevin was more than a keeper. He was a prized gem, and Ava was all in to keep her eye on the prize.

Chapter Four

Kevin made it through his first official gathering with Ava's family after three full months of dating. The family was welcoming and inviting, and there didn't seem to be any crazies among the group. Her mother had a pushiness about her, but she was sweet. Could this one day be his mother-in-law? Or was this just the beginning of her pushy ways, and would things go to another level if he ever did put a ring on Ava's finger?

For now they'd just enjoy dinner and a movie. Ava always looked so beautiful the simpler she dressed. He'd never tell her that. Of course he was attracted to the fancy Ava, but the woman without the makeup, wearing jeans and a T-shirt, was more relaxed and real, and he was attracted to the relaxed and real. That's what he saw tonight. It'd be hard to keep his hands off of her.

But he would. On the straight and narrow was where he wanted to stay. If all worked out and Ava did turn out to be the one, there'd be plenty of time for him to put his hands on her. Indulging before they were married would threaten their relationship. He had been there and done that, and he wasn't interested in doing that again or defying God's Word.

He missed doing the couple thing for the past two years, and as he clasped her smooth hand, a tingling sensation shot through his body. His pull to her was genuine. Ava had a hold on his heart, as well as other things.

"I haven't been to the movies in a long time. Thank you for bringing me." Ava smiled that gorgeous smile.

"Thank you for coming with me, Ms. Lady." He gripped tighter on her fingers as they walked into the movie theater. "I love spending time with you, so I'm glad we got a chance to do this."

She raised his hand to her mouth and kissed it gently. "Me too."

"I know I've been busy at work and distracted lately with family stuff, so thank you for putting up with me."

"Of course." She rubbed his arm. "I love you."

Tingles again. "I love you too." He gave her a peck on her forehead.

They entered the theater and headed to the standing machine by the box office. Kevin pulled out his credit card and swiped it. The ticket dispenser printed their tickets and he scooped them up.

"Don't you think ahead." Ava tightened her grip on his hand.

"Well, you know how movie theaters are: packed! Would you like any popcorn or something to drink?"

"Some popcorn would be nice, but a small bag. And a bottle of water please."

"A small bag? I want popcorn too."

They shared a laugh.

"Okay, but you're eating most of it."

"Oh, Ava, don't tell me you're watching your girlish figure. What did I tell you about that? You are perfect just the way God made you."

Ava couldn't stop smiling. "You're just wonderful. I am truly thankful that God brought us together. He knew exactly what He was doing."

After getting a large popcorn and two bottled waters they headed to the ticket taker.

"Hey, I didn't even mention what movie we're seeing."

"Kevin, I really don't care as long as I'm with you."

They entered the auditorium and quickly picked out seats. They were just perfect for Ava: not too close to the screen and directly in the middle, high enough to see the entire screen even if someone sat in front of her. Ava nestled close to Kevin, hoping the moment would last forever, as she already saw her future with him.

As the previews started, he clutched her a little tighter, cherishing the moment. Ava's eyes lit up at every preview she seemed to be interested in. Kevin missed dating and was grateful he was back in the game, especially since his teammate was Ava, an attractive woman from head to toe, and inside and out. He was more excited than he had ever been about their relationship, and he was happy. His mother would have to fall in line whether she liked it or not.

The buzz from his phone startled him. He contemplated not checking it, but with two new shaky fellas he sponsored in his drug prevention group, he couldn't ignore it. Ava leaned over away from him so he could grab the phone out of his pocket.

His mother's smiling headshot graced his phone's screen. "Ava, it's my mom. Mind if I take this outside the theater?"

"No, go 'head." Her body language didn't match her words. *Really?*

He quietly walked up the center aisle of the theater and stood outside the door. Placing the phone back to his ear, he said, "I'm here, Momma."

"I need you to come home, Kevin. Right this minute!"

"I can't, Momma. I'm on a date with Ava."

"So are you putting her before your blood relatives? I can't believe you."

He smacked his lips. "Momma, don't be silly."

She smacked her lips. "Boy, are you calling your momma silly? I know that was not intended for me."

"Of course not. I'm just saying I'm in the middle of a date, and if no one is dead or dying, then I'll come to the house after the movie is over and I drop Ava home." It was getting harder and harder to hide his irritation.

"Tweet could be dead, Kevin."

"What?" His ears perked up like a guard dog.

His mother was really reaching now. Kevin recognized this behavior in his mother. She had thrown out desperate comments of guilt before, but mentioning death was a new tactic on her part. She knew it would pull at Kevin's heartstrings.

"Well, I don't know, but she called a few minutes ago and said she was downtown somewhere, but she didn't know where she was. Then the phone cut off, and I'm really worried about her, Kev."

All kinds of inner conflict played mayhem on his emotions. Would Ava understand or be upset? Should he pay for her to take a cab home, drop her off, or invite her along for the ride? She shouldn't go, since he didn't know how long it would take to find his baby sister or what he would roll up on once he did find her. But could he ever really make it up to her if he left her alone in a theater?

As he traipsed back into the movie theater, his prayer was quick and concise. "God, please give Ava a spirit of understanding. I don't want to leave her, but I feel like I have to. Please make it go as smooth as possible."

He clasped her hand as he motioned for her to follow him. With each step he took closer to the exit, he hoped for more courage to rise up in him, and he said another prayer for the right words.

Once they got out of the auditorium and into the walkway, he caressed her face as he spoke softly. "Ava, baby, I need to go."

She stepped back as wrinkles appeared in her frown. "You need to go?" *This can't be real. Lord, are you testing me?*

Fear of Ava's anger causing a scene ran through his mind, but he couldn't run from the issue. "I know this is not what either of us wanted or expected, but my mom said Tweet called saying she didn't know where she was. Momma wants me to go look for her."

Ava forcefully tucked her arms. "Again?"

"I know. And that's why I apologized earlier. My family issues can get hectic with the worst timing."

The words Ava really wanted to say wrestled with the tip of her tongue. She held them in for fear of showing Kevin her crazy side too early. It had been three months, but this would be their first fight. She had just gotten comfortable with him and didn't want to run him off, but how could he even think about leaving her by herself at the movies? This superman complex his mother put on him was ridiculous.

Tweet was grown, and if she wanted to run the streets, there was nothing Kevin could do to stop her. She'd have to want it bad enough to even begin the process of kicking her habit. As a recovering addict turned drug counselor, Kevin should have known that all too well. Ava guessed this particular addict and her addiction hit too close to home for him. His home.

Ava sighed. "Well, I guess you gotta do what you gotta do. I can take a cab home."

"Cab?" Shaking his head, he said, "No. You ain't taking a cab. I can drop you off at home before I go on my search."

At least he knew the right way to handle it. "Okay, that's fine." Ava wanted to hide her true disgust, but her emotions had always lived on her sleeve, shoulder, face, and everywhere else. Her body language on the car ride home would surely read disappointment. She knew he was a family man, and that was one of the many things she loved about him, but if he was always running to Tweet's aid, would Ava and Kevin ever really get to know each other? *Will he run off at his mother's beck and call if we're having a nice dinner at an expensive restaurant?*

Reluctantly, Ava walked toward the exit, followed by Kevin. As they walked to the car, there was no hand holding, or even walking with each other. Kevin was too busy trying to keep up with her. He knew she was upset, but she would just have to understand. *God will give her the understanding,* he prayed silently.

When they reached the car, Kevin walked directly to the passenger's side door to open it for Ava, but she instinctively reached for the door handle, blocking Kevin from opening the door. Once they both were in the car, Ava was biting her tongue from speaking her true feelings. Instead, once Kevin turned the ignition on, she turned the radio on and sat in silence all the way to her apartment complex. As soon as he pulled into a parking space and the car stopped, Ava hopped out of the car.

Kevin hustled to catch up with her and walk her to the door. He grabbed her hand, firm and stiff, and was barely able to hold a grip on it. She wasn't feeling him right then and wanted him to know it. Her peck on his cheek was short and not so sweet.

"I'm sorry, baby. I really am." His deep voice was still a turn-on, but she wasn't feeling that either right then.

She patted his chest and looked in his eyes. "I'm sorry too." *Sorry this may not work!*

In his eyes, she read, "Hope you will be able to forgive me," but Ava couldn't address that statement at that point; she was too busy keeping her mouth shut. She closed the door, saying good-bye to his handsome face.

The Lord helped to keep her mouth closed to what she really wanted to say—for the moment, anyway. She wasn't sure how much longer she could keep her mouth sealed to the stuff between her and Kevin that she didn't agree with. She'd do her best to adhere to the Holy Spirit's lead where their issues were concerned, but she couldn't make any promises. Not allowing Kevin in on how she felt, with him dropping everything when it came to his family, was giving her a headache. She continued to let the Holy Spirit lead her to an understanding.

Chapter Five

Ava and Dr. Glory had become great friends over the past three months that she'd been dating Kevin. Ava dropped the "Doctor" from Glory's name, although it was hard to do, as they started spending time together outside of the counseling center.

On today's menu: much-needed pedicures. The soothing sounds of the flowing fountain, the background for the modern khaki and warm brown décor colors, relaxed Ava's posture into her massage chair as she and Glory sat side by side. When they hung out, Ava always felt obligated to allow Glory to speak first. She had listened to Ava's problems and issues for over a year. Ava wanted to be there for her as well and return the favor. Plus, she didn't want their friendship and the time they spent together to turn into a counseling session.

"So how are things going with you, girl?" Ava asked as she pushed her head deeper into the chair's headrest.

Glory put her phone down and closed her eyes, adjusting her shoulders in her pedicure chair. "Well, things are going."

"That doesn't sound too good." Ava didn't want to pry but figured Glory would share if she wanted to. Or, more importantly, if she needed to. Being able to get it off her chest and confide in someone who cared about her: that was one of the items Glory taught Ava in their sessions together. Getting it out and having others praying for you was an important step in getting back on the right track. Ava would be Glory's listening ear and praying friend.

She took a deep breath. "I know. Greg and I aren't seeing eye to eye and have been arguing a lot lately. Well, a little more than lately. It's constant."

"Couples argue." Ava noticed how focused her nail tech was—almost too much, as she cut away the dead skin from her heel. As long as no pain was felt, Ava could be at ease in the chair. "You told me once that it was healthy and natural to talk about it."

"Yeah, but when things get as heated as he and I have been lately, and the kids are hearing and seeing it, it's not healthy for anyone. I don't want them to think this is in any way normal."

"Oh." Ava tasted the sweet floral taste of the wine one of the techs had handed to her on her way over to another client.

Glory sat up and cocked her neck toward Ava. "You know what Hannah asked me the other night?"

"What, girl?"

"Are her mommy and daddy getting a divorce?"

The corners of Ava's mouth turned down but were quickly counteracted by the massaging moves of her nail tech. *Perfect timing.*

"Yep. That's when I knew we were doing way too much," Glory said with sadness in her face.

"What'd you say to her?"

"I told her Mommy and Daddy are just having a difficult time right now, but she didn't have to worry about us getting a divorce. It satisfied her for now, I think, but if we continue in this way . . . I don't know."

"And your li'l men? Have they asked anything about it?"

"Girl, they're fine." Glory chuckled. "Almost oblivious to what's going on. They're nine-year-old twins going on thirty-nine, and they are both sweet, but Hannah is more sensitive and emotional. She's the one who takes care of all of us."

What were the right words to say? Glory had been there for her so many times, but Ava was unsure about her own advice, as her history proved to be a bit shaky. She decided to just be a listening ear. "Yep." Ava grinned. "Hannah is sweet like that."

Seeming like she was out of energy, Glory took a long, deep breath. "How are you and Kevin doing?"

"We're good." Ava glanced down at her freshly cleaned feet. "It's his mother I'm not too sure about."

"Oh, yeah? What's the problem?"

Counseling session on. "Well, I met her for the first time the other night, and she was very unpleasant, to say the least. It wasn't nearly as welcoming as I hoped it would be."

"How so?" Glory asked behind intense eyes.

Rubbing her hands together, Ava said, "She was just plain cold. Even turned down prayers I offered for his baby sister."

Glory shrugged her shoulders. "Yeah, but I know Kev, and he didn't let her get away with acting like that, did he?"

"No, he called her on it, but it still made me feel uncomfortable. I mean, I'm no fool. I know she knows the circumstances under which we met. In her eyes, even though I was there to see you, I was one of his patients at the center and in all sorts of relationship turmoil." Ava closed her eyes. "But I'm not in that place anymore, and he and I really care about one another. Our relationship is building nicely."

"Well, don't worry about it too much. At least right now anyway. Kev doesn't do anything unless he wants to, and I know he won't kick you to the curb because of his mother's feelings. He is and always has been his own person, so I wouldn't concentrate on the negative. Keep in the positive."

Ava huffed. "That's good to know, but Mr. His-Own-Person cut out on our date early last night, before the previews were even finished."

"What?" Glory opened her eyes only to scrunch her face. "What? Why?"

"His mom called." Ava rolled her neck, reliving the moment. "Wanted him to go look for Tweet. Again."

"Yeah, I know his sister takes up a lot of his time. He's trying to save her by himself, and to me, it just doesn't seem like she wants to be saved. It's sad but true. There's nothing anyone can do about that. He loves his sister and would do anything to save her from her destructive behavior."

"That's what I said. I didn't want to sound insensitive. He's going to wear himself out, which would in turn make our relationship suffer. Is this what my life will continue to be like if we stay together? A rude mother-in-law, and a sister-in-law who gets more of his time than I do? When will I get all of his attention?"

"I know it seems that way, Ava, but I believe it'll get better. Kevin cares about you and will do what it takes to make you happy. He's one of the good ones. Trust me." She giggled.

"What?" Ava was confused by Glory's chuckle.

"Oh, nothing. That's what I used to think about Greg."

"He is still a good one, Glory, and I know you guys will work it out." Ava patted Glory's hand. "I'm sure of it."

Ava offered encouragement but wasn't 100 percent sure it helped any. The couple had been on opposing sides for a while. Greg was still out of work, while Glory's stress about everything falling on her shoulders seemed to be getting the best of her.

For the duration of the pedicure session, they sat in silence, relishing the foot scrubs and massages, along with the complimentary red wine. *Sometimes when life is too hard to try to figure out, the best thing is to just sit back and wait to see what God is going to do.*

Ava's feelings for Kevin were real. Glory's love story she shared with Greg was a beautiful one. The bumps in their roads right now seemed to be just that: bumps. Ava believed that, with God's help and leading, they'd clear them with ease.

Even though it didn't feel like that at the moment, she knew the Lord could turn the situation around with the snap of His finger. He'd done it so many times before. She just hoped He'd get to snapping sooner rather than later. She didn't know how long she could wait.

Chapter Six

Kevin loved going into work every day. New opportunities to help those in need arose daily. He'd been an addict for ten and had now been clean for eleven. He wanted to give back like so many had done for him.

Why couldn't he help Tweet though? It was embarrassing to be able to help recovering addicts at the Christian Counseling Center, but not be able to help an addict in his own immediate family. His focus would have to stay on the positive, and on how many people he'd helped to get and stay clean. Tweet would come around. He'd just stay in prayer and do what he could to keep her off the streets.

"Good morning, Kev." Glory stood there with a half smile at the makeshift coffee bar that served as the center common area in the CCC.

"Morning." He didn't dare put the word "good" in front of it. Kevin hadn't talked to Ava since he abruptly ended their date at the movies. He planned to call her during his lunch hour and hoped things went well, so it would be a good morning. If Ava could truly forgive him, it'd be a good day as well.

Glory brushed his shoulder. "Doing all right today?"

"I'm good, Ms. Lady. And you?"

"I'm here."

Kevin smiled, seeing if the phrase "fake it 'til you make it" would work in his case. "Hey, sometimes that's all we can do. And that's a blessing."

"Yes, it is a blessing, and that's all I can do today. Been feeling overwhelmed lately. Greg and I are having our same issues."

Kevin pointed at her. "I know what you need."

Raising her eyebrows, Glory's posture perked up.

"A night out on the town." He smiled at his great suggestion. She would be able to take her mind off her current situation, and he and Ava could celebrate the making-up process.

Glory's voice went an octave higher. "A what?"

"Yep, that's it." He slapped his hand. "And don't say you can't either. Get your sister to babysit, and Ava and I will meet you guys for dinner. We can all just hang out. Cool?"

"I don't know." She hung her head.

"Come on. I know you love that man." Kevin scooted closer to her for a side hug. "Give y'all a chance to just be out and away from all the stresses and just relax and have fun."

"All right, I guess. I'm not promising that Greg will want to go though. I'll get back to you."

"Sounds good to me."

They parted ways down the halls to their respective offices. Looking from the outside into Glory and Greg's relationship, they'd always seemed to be a happy couple. They may have been in the midst of a rough patch, but Kevin believed they would come out of it. He couldn't help but think about his relationship with Ava. Knowing all relationships had their issues, he'd never want to feel so distant from her that they wouldn't be able to talk about their problems or just have a night out to hang and forget about the stressors of life.

A huge stress in his life focused on his mother. He'd have to have a long talk with her and set some new boundaries now that he was in a serious relationship.

Kevin had waited for a woman like Ava to come into his life and he wasn't going to let anyone, not even his own mother, mess up this opportunity for love.

Putting those thoughts on hold, he welcomed his first client of the day into the office. "Hey, Mike. How are you today?"

"What up, Kevin?" Mike gave him dap and a manly half hug. "I'm holding on. Six days clean so far."

"That's awesome, man. I'm proud of you. Harder than you thought, I'm sure, but it's worth it. I promise." Kevin stuck out his hand to offer his client a seat.

Rubbing his hands over his pockets, Mike stood nervously like he couldn't physically sit down. "Well, I have a confession."

"Yes. Go ahead and come out with it."

"I've been carrying around some cocaine a friend gave me for my birthday two days ago."

Hearing these words made Kevin uneasy. He needed to guide and lead instead of getting too upset with the struggling addict and lashing out at him. *Firm, but loving.* "First off, you're using the word 'friend' lightly. If this person were your friend, they wouldn't give you cocaine. They do know you're trying to quit?"

Mike shrugged his shoulders. "Yeah, I guess."

"I wouldn't call them a friend. Secondly, are you sure you haven't used yet?"

"Positive." Mike rubbed his forehead. "It's like I know I don't want to use, but I don't want to throw it away and waste it either. Nor do I want to pass it along to someone else and maybe hurt their sobriety or something. I don't know. I know I sound crazy. I just don't know what to do."

"No, you sound like a perfectly normal recovering addict—and I'm still proud of you for not using, but what I don't like is you bringing it here around other recovering addicts, including myself."

"I know, I'm sorry. I'll leave." Mike turned toward the exit.

"Not with that coke on you, you won't. Plus, your session just started." Kevin motioned him over. "We'll dispose of the coke together and move forward."

Holding his head down, Mike pulled the small plastic bag with the white powdery substance in it out of his pocket. He held on to it with a tight but careful grip.

Kevin hadn't been that close to drugs in . He counted it as a test for himself and for Mike. He was confident he would pass, but he didn't want to flirt with the temptation any longer than he had to. Mike handed him the bag. Kevin could feel the loose powder shape to the indentions his fingers made in the bag.

They walked to the men's restroom right across the hall as Kevin kept the bag out of plain sight.

"Wait." Mike stopped in his tracks.

"What?" Kevin had a feeling Mike would find a way to stall the process.

"I've never done anything like this before. I don't know if I can. It seems like such a waste. Can't I just hold on to it but not use it? I promise. I just don't want to waste it. Maybe you can put it in a safe or something so I can't get to it."

Kevin rested a hand on his shoulder. "I know how you feel, but you gotta realize the waste is how your life if turning out. You have gifts and talents you haven't even tapped into yet, but the drugs could threaten you becoming who you are truly called to be. Not to mention it's hard on your physical body as well. That's just a few good reasons. I can give you more, but the main thing is you don't want to waste any more time and energy, do you?"

"No, I don't."

"You want to see your kids, right?"

"Of course I do. They mean the world to me." Mike seemed to straighten up in a defensive posture with his chest out.

"Well, this has to be done. You can do this, and I'll help you. Let the Lord's strength inside you do it. Think of it as Him doing it and not you."

Mike remained silent behind eyes of worry as he walked with Kevin in the direction of the bathroom.

"There's a scripture that says, 'God is our refuge and strength, a very present help in trouble.' I believe that's Psalm 46:1." Kevin pushed open the restroom door. "This is a time of trouble, Mike, so the Lord is here with you."

Mike took a deep breath as he grabbed the bag of cocaine out of Kevin's hand. "You're right. I can do this. I can do this. God is with me."

They traipsed into the handicapped stall. Mike knelt down and shook the powder out of the bag. He then stood and flushed the toilet. Both of them watched the cocaine swirl down in a circular motion. Kevin was relieved, while Mike was seemingly sad to be rid of the tempting substance.

Mike held up the bag in the light. "Do you know how bad I want to rub my finger on the inside of this bag and wipe my finger over my gums? What is wrong with me? Why does this have such a hold on me?"

"Nothing is wrong with you. You are an addict and that's our thought process, but you're going to throw that bag away, and then we're going to go back in my office and talk about where to go from here."

Slowly stepping out of the stall like a reluctant, small child, Mike did as he was told.

"Now wash your hands. For one, to make sure no remnants of it are on your hands, and two, let this be a spiritual and mental washing. You're washing your hands of this drug and all it has done to you and has caused you to lose."

Kevin washed his hands as well, washing away the experience of being so close to the drug he once cherished. As they traveled back to the office, Kevin reflected on how God had seen him through once again like He always did. He was thankful, and vowed to use the situation when talking about his personal testimony.

Sitting down on the couch, Kevin grabbed his Bible. "Remember and study Psalm 46:1, but I want you to also look up and study 2 Samuel 22–23." Kevin flipped through the pages.

Mike grabbed a pad and pen from the table and wrote the scriptures down.

"The scripture in 2 Samuel reads, 'God is my strength and power, and He makes my way perfect.' Believe those words. You have God-sized strength in you, and you can do things in His power. Today was just the beginning. I knew you could do it."

"Thank you for believing in me, Kevin."

"Of course. I believe, but most importantly, you gotta believe. And remember, God always gives you a way out. He makes your way perfect. There's a reason you held on to that for two days and brought it here with you."

Mike remained silent.

"You truly didn't want to use, and you knew I'd be able to offer you the help you needed to get rid of it. A way out. Proud of you, brotha."

"I'm proud of me too. I didn't think I could do it."

"Well, you did. And now we move forward."

As they discussed setting boundaries with the people in Mike's life, Kevin knew this topic hit home all too closely. He had made the decision a long time ago to set the limits with his so-called friends who used drugs in his presence. However, now the limits that needed to be set were more familial. He made a mental note to set the boundaries in his family life, starting with his mother and finishing with Tweet.

"Thank you. I didn't think I could do it without you, Kevin. I'm glad you believe in me, even though at times I don't. Thank you, again." Mike walked to the door.

Before Mike walked through the door, Kevin said, "Mike, just remember I'm always here for you. Anytime, just call me or stop by."

"Thanks again. Will do. I feel that I can actually do this now."

"Will I see you tomorrow?"

"You sure will, my brotha." Mike exited the office with a sense of hope.

Kevin quickly sent Ava a text just to let her know how sorry he was: Just wanted to apologize again for the movies the other night. I will make it up to you. Love, Kev.

Ava was a priority in his life, and he needed to behave as such before he lost her. Losing the woman in his life was something that he wasn't prepared to do, even if that meant setting stern boundaries with his mother.

Chapter Seven

Ava checked her cell. A lone text message from Toni was on her phone. While she was in the shower, she just knew Kevin would call. Why didn't he? Yes, she could call him, but she didn't want to chase after him. She wanted to be sure he wanted to do some of the chasing too.

If it were up to her, Ava would talk to him all day. His voice calmed her, and their conversations were meaningful and fun. He was definitely the reason she was all smiles lately, and it felt good.

Toni's message read: Lost the address of Rene's new office. Please send again. Thanks! See u soon.

After Ava sent her the address, she continued to get dressed. Excited to see her brother as he and his friend, Paul, would help with the big stuff, and Ava and Toni would help with the decorative part of the move, she felt Rene's excitement of a new beginning.

As she packed a few of her new delectable creations from her catering menu for their lunch break, thoughts of Kevin swirled around in her mind. His smile, his laugh, and his loving, sweet words. He answered on cue.

Her phone buzzed. The words in his text spoke to her heart. His apology for the movie fiasco a second time was even sweeter. He understood that she was upset, and he still was thinking of the situation enough to apologize again. It meant he was paying attention.

What had she done to deserve a man of his caliber? If anything, she believed she had done everything in her power to never get a good man, period, but God was a God of forgiveness and love, and He had deposited an enormous amount of both into Ava's life. The evidence of her faith was her being blessed with Kevin in her life. So, she would try not to analyze the relationship too closely, but just enjoy the path they were on together.

By the time Ava arrived at Rene's office space, everything was in full swing. Alex and Paul were moving a loveseat from one side of the room to the other as Rene directed their steps, already in boss mode in her new spot. Rene had already done quite a bit of work and decorating on her own. Matching tulip paintings hung over the couch in the waiting area. A glass wall separated the front from Rene's office, where Ava could see her degrees residing over her desk. Lastly, she had set up a small coffee station, with a variety of creamers included.

When Ava's eyes met Rene's, she jumped with excitement in the air, "Yay, Ava's here. Come here, girl. I have so much to show you."

"Hey, sis." Alex opened his arms for a big hug.

"Good to see you, bro. I've missed you." Ava shared a big embrace with her only sibling.

"I've missed you too, sis. And your niece misses you too." That familiar smile Ava loved displayed itself on Alex's proud-papa face.

"I will be by to see her tomorrow after church. Cool?"

"Of course."

Paul, as handsome as ever, sauntered over to her. "Hey, Ava."

"What's up, Paul?" The strong, intoxicating smell of his cologne made him even more attractive. It was only a few short months ago when Ava fantasized about hooking up with Paul, but now, thoughts of Kevin replaced all of those fantasies. Paul was a good man and good-looking man, and Ava knew he'd make some woman very happy one day. She would concentrate on the one God had making her happy.

Alex took the bags out of her hands and placed them on the table. "What did you bring us, sis?"

"A little something I threw together. A smoked salmon, cream cheese, and caper casserole with some fried cabbage, complete with smoked bacon and onions."

"Mmm, that all sounds good. Don't know if I can wait 'til lunch." He chuckled.

Alex had always been Ava's biggest supporter of her catering ventures, and her most faithful taste tester. His encouraging words kept her focused on her end goal of one day opening her own restaurant. Her mother's reservations about Ava being an entrepreneur were placed on the back burner, as Alex continued to help Ava believe her dream would come true. She loved him for that and so many other things.

Paul threw his arm around Rene. "Babe, don't you think we're gonna need some champagne to go with this beautiful-sounding lunch and, of course, to toast your new spot when we're done with everything?"

Wait, what? Did he just call Rene "babe"? Oh, yes, the fellas needed to go make a champagne run, so Ava could get to the bottom of this. "Yes, we do. Grab some extra plates and napkins, too, while y'all are out. Toni may bring Eric with her."

Rene smiled at Paul. "Yes, I guess we do."

Paul picked up his keys from the table. "Okay, babe. We'll be back. Text me if you think of something else."

Ava couldn't wait for the door to close behind the guys before she started in on Rene. "Girl, are you dating Paul or something?"

Rene's Kool-Aid smile answered for her, but she went ahead and obliged Ava. "Yes."

"And you didn't tell me?"

Rene's head fell. "Well, I didn't want to get my hopes up only to be wrong again."

"You know I can understand that, but I'm your best friend." Could the tainted history between them have held Rene back from divulging her new significant other to Ava?

Rene looked away. "I know. I just wanted to be sure."

"Sooo?"

"Well, things have been going great. He got my number from your bighead brother."

"Mmm." Ava got more comfortable in her chair, like listening to a story by the campfire.

"And we've been talking ever since. We've only been exclusive for about a month, but you know we've known each other since high school, so it's been cool to build on that friendship." Rene resembled a teenager talking about her first boyfriend. "We went on our first date last Saturday."

"Okay. What'd y'all do?"

"Nothing big. Just a simple dinner and great conversation at that new Italian restaurant downtown."

Reaching out to pull Rene into a hug, Ava said, "I'm so happy for you, girl. You deserve a good man, and Paul's one of the best."

Ava knew this all too well. She never let her brother in on her feelings, but there was a period of time when she imagined, hoped, and sincerely wanted Paul to end up being the man on her arm for the rest of her life. That wasn't the case now.

She'd had it all worked out, since he was practically family. He and Alex had been best friends since their freshman year in high school, so they'd all been friends for over fifteen . If nothing else, she knew she'd have her family's approval.

However, setting all of that aside to focus on Kevin, and on Rene receiving the real man she deserved, was a priceless trade-off. Ava's insecurities and issues got in the way of Rene's last relationship, and Ava would steer clear of anything that even had the appearance of drama.

God blessed all of them in His own way. Toni had remarried her best friend. Rene explored a relationship with a man of God who would treat her like the prize she was, and Ava was in love with the type of man she had been waiting for. Even though she wasn't totally happy with him at the current moment, since they hadn't talked since the movie incident, all was still well. She had never felt that way about a man before, and no one could tell her Kevin wouldn't be hers for the rest of her life. All was on schedule—but knowing how Kevin's mother felt about her, how long would their situation and relationship stay that way?

Chapter Eight

Nerves rose in Ava's belly as she waited for Kevin to come and pick her up for his mother's sixtieth birthday party at her house. Kevin and his two older sisters planned the party with family and close friends in mind. Ava was glad to be included, but wasn't sure how her presence would be received. How their last meeting played out kept running through Ava's mind. But this was a party, and there'd be many buffers between her and his mother. Plus, Kevin wanted her there, so she was there. Hopefully, the vase of bright flowers she brought for the guest of honor would help to smooth things over.

By the time Kevin arrived to Ava's third-floor apartment, she couldn't wait any longer. Granted, the last time she saw him he had ended their date early to tend to his mother's request, but he had apologized, and she had missed him and couldn't wait to wrap her arms around his neck.

His stretched-out wingspan always welcomed her in a place of familiarity and comfort. She loved it there.

Before he could knock on the door, Ava opened the door to greet him. "Oh, how I've missed you." His warm embrace made her feel even better about seeing his mother again.

"I've missed you too. Are you all set to go?"

"Ready as I'll ever be." Ava closed her apartment door and locked it. She took hold of his hand and interlocked her fingers with his as they strolled to the car. Ava couldn't stop smiling.

On the ride over, Ava could barely hear what Kevin was talking about due to the colorful daydreams that entered her head. She imagined sharing the rest of her life with him, as they would ride together, spend time together, and grow together. Loving being by his side, she desired to be there for the rest of her days on earth.

"Ava?"

She jerked her head out of her daydreams. "Yes, babe?"

"Where were you just now?" He tapped her thigh.

Chuckling, she said, "Sorry. Just thinking about something."

"Care to share?"

She looked away from him and out the window. "Not really. It's embarrassing."

"Now, Ava, you know you don't have to ever be embarrassed, baby."

"I know, but it's girlie stuff. But don't worry, it's all good stuff."

He snickered. "Okay, I guess as long as it's good stuff then I'll leave you alone." He cleared his throat as he pulled in front of his mother's house. "For now."

The now happy couple trekked up the walkway to the front door of his mother's house.

A tall, thin woman opened the door and hugged Kevin tightly. "Hey, bro."

He squeezed his sister and then stepped back. "Hey, Martha. This is my Ava."

My Ava? Oh, yeah, that sounds good. Tonight's going to be a good night.

"Yep, I heard Kev was dating somebody new." She spoke from behind bushy eyebrows. "Momma filled me in about you."

Was that a dig? Not sure how to take his sister's statement, Ava wanted to take the high road, but sarcasm had always been a confidant of hers. "Well, nice to meet you too."

"Mmm. Same to you." The air filled with Martha's judgment of Ava.

Kevin stuck out his hand. "As you can see, Ava, Martha and my mother are just alike."

"What's that supposed to mean?" Martha stomped her foot as she folded her arms.

He cocked his head and smiled. "You know exactly what that means."

Rolling her eyes, she waved at him. "Whatever, boy."

Another woman who shared the siblings' facial features sauntered up. Her hair was a rougher texture than her sister's. She wasn't quite smiling, yet not frowning, resembling a small child who was made to go somewhere she didn't particularly want to go to. Her face said it all: not inviting.

Kevin put his hand on her shoulder. "Ava, this is my other sister, Mary."

"Nice to meet you." Ava tried it again in a sweeter tone and stuck her hand out, hoping for a better welcome.

Mary stuck out her hand, but lightly shook Ava's hand as if someone forced her to perform the simple greeting.

"There's my son," Kevin's mother called to him from the kitchen.

He kissed Ava on the cheek and said, "I'll be right back."

Ava would have rather walked and stood in a corner, but she went ahead and attempted to be social with those who didn't seem like they wanted to be to social with her. "So, Martha and Mary. That's cute."

"Cute? I don't know if that's the word for it." Martha huffed as she tossed her thick black hair back out of her face, spewing enough attitude for the both of them.

Ava couldn't seem to say the right thing to anyone in that house. She wanted to step back and politely get out of harm's way.

Martha took the vase out of Ava's hands. "Flowers, huh? For a sixtieth birthday?" She cut her eyes at her sister. "Now, that's cute." Her smile was tainted by the hint of sarcasm.

The two giggled as they walked away. Was Ava meeting the family too soon? She stood firm in her spot in the room, biting her lip for fear of following the two women and saying what she really wanted to say. Kevin, sweet and thoughtful, must have been like his father. His dad had passed almost two before, and Ava was certain that Kevin's personality and manners must've come from him. No doubt his two older sisters shot out with the manners of their mother.

Ava slouched over to an area of the room where few people stood. She kept her eyes on the interaction between her man and his siblings. At that moment, she couldn't see herself ever fitting in with the tight, judgmental group. She had Kevin's attention, but she wasn't sure she was out to capture the hearts of his family. Ava had already learned to appreciate herself for who God made her to be, and if they didn't like her, so be it. She had best friends who were like sisters, and a sister-in-law she was already close with. She didn't need any more, that's for sure.

The front door swung open, and a small, thin young woman dressed in baggy jeans and a black hooded sweatshirt stepped over the threshold. Standing there, rough around the edges and looking a bit tipsy, she said, "Tweet's in the house! And it's Momma's birthday. Yeah, let's get our party on, fools." She threw her hands up like she was the hype man on stage at a concert. "Get it, big sixty! Yay, yay! Get it, big Momma!"

The partygoers seemed taken aback, looking as if they weren't sure what to do. Kevin rushed over to her and put his arms around her, trying to remove her to another room. "Tweet. Come on. Let's go in the kitchen for a moment."

She wrestled her body loose from his arms. "Why we leaving, Kev? I'm here for the party. Where the music at?"

Kevin got another grip on her arm and leaned in to whisper something into her ear. "Tweet, you're not yourself. Please, before you embarrass Momma."

Tweet shrugged her shoulders and pushed him away from her body. "I'm not gonna embarrass anybody. I'm just here to celebrate Momma's big sixtieth birthday. I can't party with y'all? Is that what you are saying?"

In a firm voice, he said, "It seems like you've already been partying."

Ava moved over toward them, since no one else seemed to be.

He pushed Tweet into the kitchen. Ava followed.

"Tweet, I know you didn't come up in Momma's house high. What is wrong with you?"

She sat down at the kitchen table and took a deep breath. "A lot."

"Do you need me to do anything, Kevin?" Ava inched his way.

Tweet frowned up her face. "Who's this?"

"No, Ava. It's okay." He turned to Tweet. "This is Ava, my girlfriend."

"She's beautiful, Kevin. You doing good for yourself, brotha." She chuckled as she patted him on the back.

"Thanks, but you ain't so hot right now." He grabbed his keys off the counter and turned to Ava. "In fact, baby, we can do something. Let's take her to go get some coffee or something. Will you drive?"

Ava nodded. "No problem. Whatever you need me to do."

His mother came in and went straight to Tweet and gave her a hug, holding her tightly for what seemed like an hour. "Baby, it's so good to see you. I know you're not yourself, but I'm glad you're here. I've been worried about you."

"Momma, Ava and I are going to take Tweet to go get some coffee and sober up."

"What do you mean 'Ava and I'? I done told you how I feel about outsiders in our business. This is a family issue, and she's not our family." His mother rolled her neck like a teenager with a bad attitude.

"We don't have time for that right now, Momma." He handed the keys to Ava. "We're going to get her sober and bring her back after everyone leaves."

His insistence with his mother turned Ava on, but she needed to focus on the problem at hand. She could revisit those feelings later.

"I don't wanna go, Momma. I wanna stay and kick it with you and your peoples. But I don't want to mess up your party either." Tweet broke out into tears as she fell into a chair at the small kitchenette table. "I'm sorry, Momma. I'm sorry. I just ruin everything for everyone."

Her mother rubbed her head. "It's okay, baby. We're gonna get you the help you need. And never forget—we love you no matter what."

"Well, let's go, you two." Tweet slapped the table and stood. "I got to get to know my future sister-in-law." She interlocked her arm with Ava's and guided her toward the door. Kevin's mother seemed to cringe at her daughter's words, or Ava could've just imagined her showing displeasure. Either way, Ava wasn't interested in pleasing them anymore. She would not bend over backward for folks who wanted nothing to do with her.

Tweet may have been under the influence of drugs, but so far she had been the only one who was the most welcoming of Ava's presence into the family. Neither Martha nor Mary had come to see about their baby sister. Why didn't they come to their sister's aid? Ava felt sorry for her in a way, as Tweet seemed to be hurting and alone, but Ava understood that she didn't know the whole story. When Kevin felt the need to share, she'd be there to listen.

However, with all she had been through in her life, she would give Tweet her full consideration as she learned more about her and her story. Ava hoped to start a great foundation for their future relationship, whatever that turned out to be: friend, sister-in-law, and, probably most importantly, ally.

Chapter Nine

Kevin didn't know how to feel about Ava sitting at the table, getting a front-row seat of his sister high off of whatever her current drug of choice was. He was grateful for Ava's support, though, and the fact that she didn't run the other way after the less-than-favorable scene at his mother's house impressed him more than anything. Some women he had dated in the past would get a glimpse of his family's drama and issues and would burn off in the other direction as soon as possible. But Ava stayed.

IHOP was his favorite spot to take his sponsees and sober them up when needed. He could enjoy great pancakes while they sipped coffee and explained their slip-up. He needed to now do the same for his sister. Excited that his girlfriend and sister were meeting, he wasn't sure this was the best circumstance for them to get to know each other, but it was too late. They were there now, and Ava's supportive ways were a wonderful thing to see.

The booth seemed to swallow Tweet's little body up as she sat silently across from the couple, sipping coffee. Kevin caressed Ava's hand. She looked like she wanted to say something but wasn't sure what to say. She still didn't want to intrude on such a family issue, but she couldn't just sit there staring out the window.

After taking a drink from her glass of water, Ava cleared her throat and said, "So, Tweet. How'd you get that nickname?" She hoped her question would ease the tension of how they met.

"Nickname?" Tweet frowned. "Girl, that's my real name. Our parents were hippies."

"Oh, really. That's nice." Ava leaned back into the booth, thinking maybe that wasn't the best way to start the conversation.

Kevin chuckled, wanting to let Ava in on the joke before she scooted out of there without looking back.

"No, not really." Tweet put her hands up and shook her head. "But I almost had you. Right?"

"Yep, you almost had me," Ava admitted sheepishly with laughter.

Her warm, hearty laugh comforted Kevin. He loved to make her laugh and smile. All was good when the woman he loved was happy. He hoped he'd be able to keep her that way.

Tweet went on. "I'm not proud of it, but when I was younger, I used to have some weird obsession with birds and would chase them around in our yard, yelling, 'Tweet, tweet, tweet.' I was a hot mess."

"Girl, please. We all did stuff we aren't proud of when we were little. That's a very fitting and cute nickname." Ava seemed comfortable in Tweet's presence. That was more than Kevin could say for most people. He appreciated her nonjudgmental demeanor, and it seemed his baby sister did too.

"Yep, my real name is Kaleeya." She flexed her brow. "I like Tweet better."

"Kaleeya. That's pretty." Ava smiled. "Tweet is easier to remember though."

They shared a laugh as the pancakes arrived, led by the scent of warm butter and hot, fluffy goodness. Kevin's mouth watered with all the senses that flirted with his disposition at that point. He couldn't wait to get to that first bite.

Tweet, on his same page, pushed her coffee cup aside and immediately went into slapping the butter on each side of the three-stack of buttermilk pancakes. She then grabbed the syrup and drizzled the sweet goodness all over the hotcakes. Sliding the knife through the fluffy mountain, she cut a large sliver off and stuffed it in her mouth. Looking up, smiling, she stared at her brother.

"Slow down, girl, before you choke." Kevin figured she was hungry, but he wasn't looking to show off his Heimlich maneuver skills to anyone.

"I can't help it." She wiped the piece of pancake that got away off of her chin. "I don't remember the last time I ate."

Tilting his head, Kevin asked, "Don't remember, or can't remember?"

Tweet smacked her lips. "What's the difference?"

"Don't get an attitude with me. I'm just trying to assess the full situation."

"I know, bro, but you don't have to worry about me." She swallowed a large bite. "I'm just fine."

"Your definition of 'fine' and mine are probably two different things." Kevin forced his voice to stay at a calm level. He wasn't about to get into an argument with his little sister in public, and especially in front of Ava. As she rubbed his back, he was thankful she was there to calm him.

"Ooh, these are so good." Tweet licked her lips as she finished chewing, only to guzzle half of her milk down.

"I'm sure they are, but are you gonna come up for air?" Ava giggled.

"I will once I'm done." She stared down at her plate. "I'll be honest with you, bro. I don't think I've eaten in about three days. I was too busy with other stuff."

Kevin sat straight up and placed his cloth napkin on the dark wooden table. "Other stuff like what?"

"Well, you know I can't stop smoking weed. That'll just never happen. And I have a love affair with coke, but a friend of mine introduced me to speed, and that wasn't a bad high at all. That's what I took a hit of before Momma's party. I was gonna be the hype man for the party." She looked down as she mashed her fork into her eggs. "Until you stopped me."

"Tweet, are you kidding me?" His anger started to seep out as she acted like it was a joke to use when he had spent all his free time trying to keep her clean. Ava didn't seem too disturbed after hearing about Tweet's drug abuse. If she was bothered by it, she put up an excellent front. She occasionally made eye contact as if she was truly worried. Her sincere concern made him realize how much she cared. Ava could've been anywhere, but she wasn't. She was with him, by his side. Her support settled his anger. "I thought you were sincerely wanting to quit this time."

"I know I said that, but you've been there. You know what it's like." She awkwardly sunk down into her seat. "Oops, did I say too much?"

"No, you didn't say too much. Ava already knows everything." He grabbed Ava's hand and kissed it. "And she loves me anyway."

"I sure do." Ava returned the same show of affection on his hand.

Tweet rocked her head back and forth. "Well, that's a first." She turned to Ava. "He must really like you. He's usually like a locked treasure chest. That's why his other relationships didn't work out."

"Thanks, Tweet, for telling all my business." Kevin rolled his eyes.

Ava glanced at him. "I'm glad to know I'm the first woman you've confided in. I think it's sweet."

Kevin leaned in closer toward his baby sister. "So, you haven't eaten in days. Where have you been staying?"

Tweet let out a deep sigh. She pushed both of her hands through her hair and hung her head. "Around. You know—here, there, wherever."

"Where have you been staying?" Kevin added more bass in his voice, sounding like their father.

"You know, here and there. At a few of my homies' cribs. Stayed a night or two at the shelter, but I only had to spend one night on the street when the shelter was too full."

He shook his head in disgust. "On the street, Tweet?"

"Well, I had to. I told you the shelter was full and I had no place to go."

"Tweet, you have places you can stay. My house, Momma's, Martha or Mary's. I can go on—"

She put her hand up. "Well, don't. You know Martha and Mary do not care what happens to me. I burned that bridge a long time ago. And I didn't want to bother you or Momma. I was a mess that night anyway. It was better I stayed away."

"How so?" His anger softened into concern.

She looked away. "I tried to smoke crack that night. It was my first time. I didn't know how I was gonna react."

Kevin's head fell. "Are you wanting to have your life go to complete hell? I love you unconditionally, Tweet. You know that, but you gotta see what you're doing to yourself. I know. I was there, and I know what that did to my life." He touched her forearm that rested on the table. "I don't want to see you go through that. I'm here to help you, Tweet. I want you to love yourself and want better for yourself."

"You turned out all right, Kev." Tweet puffed up her shoulders. "I'll be fine. You don't have to worry about little ol' me. I'll be okay."

"I'm serious, girl." He added a sternness to his voice. "I love you and care deeply about you."

"Just give me a little more time. It's harder than I thought." She ran her fork down through the syrup on her plate like a small child listening to a boring parent's lecture. "I'll get clean. I promise. I will, one day."

Kevin twiddled his thumbs. He didn't want it to seem like he was ignoring Ava, but he needed to get to the bottom of Tweet's situation and get the wheels turning on some solutions. "I know you will, and I'm going to help you as many times as you need me to. That's a promise I will hold forever."

"You have been helping me, and I appreciate it. All of it. Even this right now is helping me. God knows I would've embarrassed Momma in the worst way."

"No, I mean some real help." He lifted Tweet's head to look into her eyes. "After we go back by Momma's and you see everyone, I'm checking you into a rehab facility. Something I should've done a long time ago. I'm just sorry I didn't do it sooner. I just was too emotionally invested in thinking I was the only who could help you. It was selfish of me. I'm sorry, Tweet. As a counselor, I should've known better. A rehab facility is the start of your recovery."

She quickly shook her head and tightened her lips. "I don't need a place like that. For your information, you can still get drugs in there, so don't think it's the best thing." She folded her arms.

"Yes, you do. And I'm not about to sit idly by and watch you destroy yourself. Besides, this facility is very strict. There are random room searches, and no one can just come in and out of the facility without a counselor present. You will have a warm bed and hot meals three times a day. It will be good for you."

Ava fidgeted with her purse as if she didn't know what to say. *Maybe a bathroom break would be good right about now.* Too late; she was already in the thick of it. She was definitely in on the family issues now, whether Kevin's mother liked it or not, and she was still by his side. If she could be there for him regardless of how messy his mess was, he'd aim to keep her by his side for the rest of his life—with or without his mom's or older sisters' approval.

Chapter Ten

Ava looked forward all week to her and Kevin's first double date with Glory and Greg. She had learned so much from Glory and valued their friendship, and she wanted to see her happy as well. With all the problems they'd had lately, Ava knew they could probably use a night out to just be together away from the stress of their current situation.

As Glory and Greg walked up to meet them in front of the restaurant, Ava was almost sure they were holding hands, which was a great sign. This would be a good night.

"What's up, my peeps?" Glory laughed at her own greeting.

"Hey, girl." Ava turned to Greg. "Great to see you again."

Kevin hugged Glory and shook Greg's hand. The foursome made small talk, exchanging updates on family and friends, as they waited to be seated. Greg's body language read much more positive than the last time Ava met him. His peaceful demeanor put her at ease where she could relax the rest of the night. Tension between one couple had the potential to mess up the flow of the other couple in their presence, but all was well.

They followed the hostess to their table. People seemed to be enjoying their food and conversations. The room was dimly lit, with a modern décor with an Asian flair. The scene was fairly uneventful, except for the busy noise that came out of the kitchen, as waiters and waitresses went in and out to pick up their orders. When they arrived at the table, Kevin pulled out Ava's chair, while Greg took his seat. Glory stood looking at him as if to transfer her words with her eyes.

Greg quickly stood. "Oh, my bad." He pulled out his wife's chair, seemingly embarrassed.

Glory nodded, smiling. "Thank you kindly."

Everyone opened their menus as the hostess gave her spiel about the night's specials.

"Everything is so expensive." Greg put down his menu. "I would've been cool at a Chili's or something."

Kevin chuckled. "I know it's a bit pricey, but I've wanted to try this place for a while and thought this would be the perfect time. Besides, I'm treating, so don't worry about it. Get want you want. It's okay. I promise."

Glory waved her hand. "You don't have to do that, Kevin." She sighed. "I don't know why you're complaining anyway, Greg. You're not paying for it. I am."

Greg cut his eyes at her. Ava wanted to disappear right then, but just avoided making eye contact with him or Glory.

"Really, it's no problem, y'all." Kevin smiled. "I want to treat, guys. I don't want you to have to worry about anything. Just enjoy the food. I hear it's great. And the atmosphere ain't too bad either." He presented the place to the table. "So let's just enjoy our evening, worry free and stress free."

"No, it's cool, Kev. Let Ms. Money Bags over here take care of it, seeing as how she doesn't mind throwing it in my face every chance she gets. Like it doesn't bother me that my wife is picking up the tab." He stood and threw his napkin on the table. "I'm gonna go out and get some air before I say something I can't take back."

Glory folded her arms, sat back in her chair, and watched him walk out on the restaurant's patio. She was fuming mad and embarrassed by his actions.

Not sure what to do, Ava thought it may be good to give Glory a place to go to take five as well. "Hey, girl, I need to go to the restroom. Come with me?"

Ava felt sorry for Greg. As far as she knew, he had been trying his best to get a job and make things work between them. She knew Glory was probably running out of patience with the situation, but she didn't have to be so harsh in front of the group. Since Ava didn't know the details and didn't want to speak on their relationship anyway, she changed their focus as they entered the restroom.

"You'll have to make time to go see Rene's new spot. She just moved into her new office building and will soon open the doors to her new practice in a little less than a month. Hopefully, you'll be able to come to the official opening."

"I'll be there." Glory sounded less than excited.

Ava kept the conversation going. "She's also dating my brother's best friend, Paul. Things are looking up for her. You know she deserves things to turn out in her favor. After all the mess I've caused in her life, I truly am happy for her."

"That's good. I'm glad for her." Glory stared into the mirror for a moment; then she wiped her face with both hands. "And how's Toni?"

"She's good. Enjoying the remarried life." Ava giggled. "I think she and Eric are doing better than they ever have. It's great to see. I know it's only been about five months or so since they renewed their vows, but they seem as happy as can be."

"Well, good. At least somebody is happy in their marriage."

Ava's distraction plan wasn't working, so she gave in. "You and Greg all right?"

"I don't know." Glory hung her head and sniffled.

Grabbing a Kleenex out of the box that sat on the marble counter in the ladies' restroom, Ava walked over to her.

Glory took the tissue and dabbed her eyes. "I know I shouldn't say some of the things I say, but lately everything he does just irritates me, and before I know it, something hurtful slips out of my mouth."

"Well, don't be so hard on yourself. Or on him. You know he's trying. If he had it his way, he'd be working the perfect job and could take care of you and the kids. Just give him some more time. I know his breakthrough is coming." Ava didn't know for sure, but knew the Man who did know. She hoped to sprinkle a little faith on her friend, who seemed to have her faith depleted and tested.

"I know." Glory's words lacked confidence and hope.

Ava gave her a hug. "It'll get better. Hold on to that."

Heading back to the table, Ava noticed that Greg hadn't made it back. Glory slowly sat down but kept her eyes on the lookout for his return.

Ava couldn't wait to be back by Kevin's side. She wanted him to be her husband. Yes, they'd have their own set of problems and arguments, like all couples, but she couldn't imagine anything coming between her and her marriage to him. She never wanted to feel like she couldn't stand to be around him like Glory felt about Greg. The hand-holding when they walked up to the restaurant must've been a "fake it 'til you make it" for Ava and Kevin's sake. It was clear they were not in a good place.

Ava never wanted to visit that place in her marriage. She desired to be married above anything else, and nothing would mess that up. Ava had waited a long time for a husband, and if Kevin, who seemed like the perfect candidate, ever did ask, she'd jump in wholeheartedly. She vowed to herself that she would do everything in her power to hold on to their bond together.

Kevin stood when they arrived.

What is he doing? Ava stepped back. "Oh, your turn to go to the restroom now?"

"No, babe. It's what I'm supposed to do when my lady returns."

She grinned. "Oh, right. Somehow I'm still not used to that at all. Thank you." Yep, she definitely wanted to walk down the aisle toward his handsome face and caring, chivalrous ways. They enjoyed each other's company, had some of the same dreams and goals, laughed together often, and it had been programmed in him before his father left the earth to be with the Lord to treat women like the prizes they were. She could definitely get used to all of the above.

Of course, it was a shame she had never experienced being treated like a lady. Ava had always settled for the same types of fools. Kevin was a nice change from the usual. He was the best boyfriend she'd ever had, and hopefully, this was the best who was saved for her last.

Chapter Eleven

Proud of his sister for actually staying at his mother's house for a couple of days in a row, Kevin showed up at his mom's house early Monday morning to make her a full breakfast. That morning, he was checking her into the Shady Grove drug and alcohol rehab center. Tweet was less than excited but was willing to go, and that was all he wanted. For now.

He wasn't sure if she had used while she was at their mother's, but the facility couldn't take her until that day, so he had no choice but to give her some freedom to do as she pleased over the weekend. His mother didn't have any complaints, so all seemed well.

"Tweet, Tweet. Let's go. Your breakfast is ready." Kevin enjoyed taking care of his little sister. He had always been taken care of and spoiled by his older sisters. He loved getting a chance to spoil his baby sister.

A minute or two later, she came bobbing down the stairs like a schoolgirl. "Thanks, bro. You take such good care of me."

"I try." He kissed her on her forehead as she sat down at the table. "And I look forward to the day you can take care of yourself."

Tweet snickered. "That may never happen. We both know that."

He slid some eggs on her plate and then dropped the plate of toast and bacon on the kitchen table. "Don't say that. You can, Tweet. Lean on God and put your trust in Him. Not in yourself. Believe me. That doesn't work."

"I can do that." She took a large bite. "I think."

"You can, baby." Her mother shuffled into the kitchen and kissed her forehead. Then she hugged Kevin. "And aren't you just the sweetest big brother ever."

"Thank you, Momma." He returned the loving gesture. "You want some eggs?"

"Yes, baby, I'll take a little. Not too much though." His mother held her forehead as she sat down at the kitchen table. "Not feeling too well this morning."

Kevin sat down by his mother. "Are you okay, Momma? Have you been taking your medication?"

"I'm fine, baby."

"I don't know, Momma. You don't look so good." He did a once-over of his mother's whole upper body. "I'm gonna call Martha and tell her to come and take you to the doctor today."

"I don't need to go to no dern doctor. I said I'm fine. I know my body better than any ol' doctor." She lifted the coffee pot in the center of the table to pour a cup. Her shaky, weak hand couldn't hold on to the grip, and the pot of coffee fell back onto the table, splattering across the table as the glass broke. "Dang it!"

Kevin rushed to his mother's aid. He picked up the big piece of glass and threw the paper towel roll at Tweet. The two cleaned up the mess together. He wasn't happy with the mess, but he liked that he and his sister were doing something together again that didn't include drug use.

After she threw away the wet paper towels, Tweet sat back down and caressed her mother's arm. "I'll go if you go, Momma."

Kevin turned to his sister. "Oh, you going, Ms. Lady. Ain't no doubt about that."

Tweet huffed. "I know. I just want Momma to go too. She needs to take care of herself."

"I will. You can tell Martha to pick me up in an hour." His mother nodded his way. "Now, go on and pray over the food, son."

He closed his eyes and lowered his head. The ladies followed suit. "Lord, we ask that you bless this meal and help it to nourish our bodies. Bless the hands that prepared it and the bodies it's going into." He paused to smile and went on. Tweet snickered. "Also, Lord, as your daughter submits to getting help with her drug issues and going into this facility, please meet her right where she's at. And whatever is going on in Momma, please remove it from her body. Amen."

Their mother couldn't contain herself. "Amen, Lord!"

"We put our trust in you, Father. We know you hold us and keep us in your hand, and you make a way when there seems to be no way. Please give her God-sized strength and walk with her through this process. We love you, Lord, and thank you in advance for the signs, miracles, and wonders we'll see you perform in her life. In Jesus' name."

"Amen," the ladies said together.

After they finished breakfast, Tweet grabbed her duffle bag of clothes, kissed her mother, and headed to the car. As his mother squeezed his neck, wearing a big smile, Kevin felt the pride she had in the fact that he was taking his sister's attempts to get sober seriously, in thought and in action.

Kevin held his mother tight. "You take care of yourself, Momma. Let me worry about Tweet."

"Okay, baby. I will."

He rubbed her back. "I'm serious, Momma. You promise?"

"Yes, son. I promise." She smiled and kissed his cheek.

Kevin returned the gesture and then bounced out the front door.

On the car ride over to the rehab center, Kevin could sense a certain sadness in his baby sister. "What you thinking about, Tweet?"

"Nothing." She tapped her leg nervously. "Just wondering if I can really do this. Do you think I can do this after all this time?"

"Try not to think of it as you doing it, but the God in you getting it done. Stay prayed up and follow all of the instructions given to you by the counselors." He tapped the wheel. "As a counselor myself, I've seen this end great, and not so great. It's those who stick to the plan and really work it that end up kicking the habit for good. You get what I'm saying?"

Tweet nodded as she stared out of her car door window, a bit hesitant in herself.

"You gotta believe in you and the God in you, and you'll be fine. And know that I believe in you, baby sis."

"Thank you, Kev. I love you."

He smiled. "I love you more."

Kevin's emotions were split. He wanted to tear up for so many reasons, but he didn't want Tweet to see him emotional as she walked through the doors of the facility, as it would probably spark a domino effect.

He still saw the little girl who'd follow him everywhere he went—even the bathroom, before he got too old and would kick her out, demanding his privacy. She'd throw a fit and then sit outside the door until he was done. It was sweet. In his eyes, she'd never grown up.

Kevin truly hated himself for introducing her to drugs. If he could go back and change the circumstances, he would, but all he could do now was do his best to get her clean and on the right track. He'd been able to guide so many of his patients to sobriety, and he would never give up on his baby sister. He understood now that he couldn't do it alone.

She could go kicking and screaming or go quietly, but he'd never lose hope. He was glad that she was choosing the latter of the two though. It made his life easier. The trip was almost too easy. In the past, she had always resisted correction or help to get rid of her addiction. Tweet lived in denial and never thought she had a problem, so opposition was always at the forefront.

Not today. Did she have a plan up her sleeve? Was she pulling the cloak over his eyes once again? He didn't want to question her willingness to go and mess up anything, so he stayed quiet. Kevin did have a plan of his own though. He would visit her every other day and stay on top of her counselors. She would know he was still there.

Plus, he was cool with the counselors at this particular facility, and they would have no problem keeping him informed about his sister's daily activities. He'd also stay prayed up on behalf of Tweet and his whole family. He wanted to will her to kick this habit once and for all.

Chapter Twelve

Ava knew her time as a juvenile probation officer was just about up. The kids' issues and offenses became more serious and dangerous as the days went on. The teens also became more defiant and rude. Her heart wasn't in it anymore. She wanted to make a difference and believed she was, but the days were becoming longer and more stressful. Ava wanted to be on her own schedule and doing what she was truly passionate about: cooking.

She wanted to pour all of her energy into her catering business and start working on her business plan to open her own restaurant. Ava had been building up her savings and was halfway to the amount the bank told her she would need to put up for the business loan. She was almost there.

Her dream of a restaurant that offered a full, enjoyable meal and experience would hopefully happen sooner rather than later. She could make a difference in people's lives by giving them a pleasant time while at her spot. Ava even explored the idea of offering tasty and healthy alternatives to some of her best creations. She was ready to start putting things into motion.

As she flipped through the piles of case paperwork on her desk, she daydreamed about how her restaurant would be set up and what the décor would look like: warm browns and colors that relaxed and soothed people, soft music, a welcoming atmosphere, and, of course, the best food. She could even have her wedding reception there for free. *Wait, where'd that come from?*

She giggled at how quickly her mind traveled to her and Kevin's wedding day. Was it too much to ask though? She and Kevin had been together almost a full six months now, and she knew God had picked him out for her. Kevin just needed to know it. *Why doesn't he know it already?*

Before she could go too far off the deep end, a knock at the door broke her train of thought. "Yes?"

A muffled voice behind the door answered, "It's me. Lisa."

Lisa worked in the records department. She was one of Ava's work friends, but she usually didn't come around too much until Fridays, when she wanted to discuss the possibility of getting to a happy hour somewhere.

"Come on in, girl." Ava closed the file in front of her as Lisa came into her office. "What's up?"

"Not much." She paused in her steps. "Are you busy? If you are, I can come back later."

"A little, but nothing that can't wait." Ava put her pen down, straightened the stack of papers she was working on, and placed them on top of the file.

Lisa tossed her red locks out of her lightly freckled face as she sat down. "I have a weird favor to ask you. I mean, nothing too extreme, but a favor that will mean a lot to me."

Not sure what to think, but curious, Ava said, "Well, come on out with it."

Lisa twiddled her thumbs as she hesitated. "I hope you don't think I'm crazy, but . . ." She took a deep breath.

Ava chuckled, shaking her head. "Just say it, girl. I'm sure whatever it is, it'll be all right."

She placed her hands on Ava's desk. "Okay, I know we haven't known each other that long, only a few months, but I have no one else to go to."

"No one else for what?" Ava started to worry. What in the world did she want?

Lisa threw her hands up. "Okay, I'll just say it."

"Please do." Ava tried to contain her irritation with the suspense of the conversation. *It better be nothing crazy!* Ava had only known Lisa for several months. They weren't close in her eyes.

"I don't have that many friends, good ones anyway. Or sisters. And I just wanted to ask if you wouldn't mind being my maid of honor?" She held her head down while she giggled, seemingly embarrassed.

"Me?"

"Yeah, well, we've gone to a couple of happy hours together and have shared about our significant others. And you know my boyfriend and I have been together for a while. We've been living together for two , so he finally asked me to marry him and, of course, I said yes." Her face grew solemn. "But like I said, I really have nobody else, and since I thought we were cool, you'd be perfect."

"Convenient" or "available" may have been better words, but not "perfect."

"Well. I . . . guess . . ." Ava lacked the perfect answer. She couldn't believe how many people she knew who shacked up yet got married before she did. Not necessarily wanting to be categorized as a hater, she couldn't help feeling mistreated and forgotten about. Ava wanted to do things the traditional way, but the end goal was the same: marriage. It just seemed like by living with the man, a woman could get there faster.

"You don't have to say anything right now. I know this is coming out of left field. I just want it to be as special as possible. My family really isn't feeling him, and I'm doing this on my own, but I would like for someone who knows me and isn't a wench to stand there with me. I would like someone there for me who only has the best intentions for me."

Ava looked into Lisa's sad eyes and put her feelings aside. Yes, Lisa had been shacking up for two , and yes, there seemed to be some family issues and red flags that Lisa wasn't paying attention to, like his slip-ups with his ex-girlfriend, baby momma drama, and lack of the ability to keep a job; but at least she was trying to do the right thing, putting an end to the shacking up for a chance at happy holy matrimony. "I don't need to think about it. I'll do it for you."

"Yay!" She stood and screamed, then covered her mouth as if she didn't know how loud she really was. "Thank you so much, Ava. This means a lot to me. But there's one more favor . . ."

"Okay, but I'm not doing a bachelorette party. I'm not entertaining any of that stripper stuff, so you will have to find someone else." Ava was stern.

"Oh, no, Ava. Absolutely not. I have found my man, and I don't want to see or be next to any other man with his clothes off."

They both let out an awkward chuckle.

"Actually, I heard you also cater, and I would love for you to do it. Of course, I will pay you for the event, and the menu is all up to you. You can surprise us. None of my guests has any allergies. Can you do it? I mean, no pressure if you don't. I totally understand. You have already made my day."

Ava sat back and said nothing. She could see Lisa's face actually contorting a bit while she waited for her answer.

"You know what, Ava? That's just too much to ask. Don't worry about it. I'll get someone else to cater." Lisa started to stand.

"Oh, no, you won't. After all, I am in the business. I will be happy to do it. And are you sure about giving me the go ahead with the menu?"

"Of course. I'm sure you will do something amazing for my day." Lisa was elated. She couldn't stop smiling.

Ava laughed at her coworker's overexcitement. "You're very welcome. I'm happy to do it for you."

"You just don't know how much of a weight has been lifted." She clasped her hands together and bowed her head toward Ava. "Thank you so much."

"What shall I wear?" Ava's mind was already heading in the direction of one of her biggest insecurities.

"Wear whatever you want. I'm just glad you'll be there." Lisa skipped around the desk to give Ava a hug. "Thank you, thank you, thank you."

"You're welcome, girl. Just tell me when and where and I'll be there."

"It's in three weeks. On Valentine's Day. I'll e-mail you the details. Thanks again." Lisa seemed to glide back out of the room.

Ava was glad to bring some joy to Lisa's life, but was this really happening? First, her crazy cousin's wedding, and now, she'd be standing at the altar for a woman she hardly knew and who hardly knew her. To top it off, someone who had been living with her boyfriend was getting married when Ava had been trying her best to walk the straight and narrow path but still wasn't walking down any aisles. Was she not doing everything right in God's eyes?

Life could be cruel at times. Ava didn't want to feel the way she did, but right at that moment that was all she could do. When would she get her day? When would her dream be fulfilled? Envy never really looked good on anybody, and she didn't want to wear it, but her emotions were all over the place. *Pray.*

"Lord, only you know what to make of me and my life. And I don't mean to be ugly, but really? I don't understand. Why is everyone getting married but me?

I'm a good person and deserve happiness too, right? I'm trying to go about things the right way, but I don't know how much longer I can hold on. I will do my best to keep putting my trust in you and hope for the best. I still believe you have a plan for me."

She couldn't offer a flashy prayer right then, but she wanted to believe the words would help. Now, within three weeks, she'd need to find a dress that fit and find a way to hide her envious feelings. Ava wasn't sure she'd be successful at either.

Chapter Thirteen

On the designated day to celebrate love, Ava stood in a small storefront church wearing her all-too-familiar fake smile. It was getting easier these days to drum up, though. As the Shacker—Ava's secret nickname for her coworker—strolled toward her husband-to-be, Ava caught Kevin staring at her. His wink sent a chill through her body. He was an attractive man. Some days she found it hard to believe that he had picked her. But he had, and he recognized her inner and outer beauty. For that, she was grateful. All the other fools before him were a waste of her time, but they did make her appreciate Kevin even more, so maybe having been in a relationship with them wasn't a total loss. The previous men in her life had done their part, and she would do hers to make and keep Kevin happy.

Ava glanced at Toni as she sat with her arm around Eric. Lisa didn't mind Ava bringing extra guests. Many of her invited guests couldn't make it, or didn't want to attend, so Ava was glad to help the Shacker out.

The ceremony, short and sweet, provided Ava with another opportunity to critique and pick apart what she did and didn't like about the decorations and wedding agenda. She wouldn't have the traditional tune playing as she walked down the aisle. Her song would be one that she and Kevin both cherished. Her sister-in-law, Elaine, would belt the song out like a professional.

Ava had everything checked off on her list of items for her wedding agenda. She just needed the date and the dude. Hopefully, Kevin was the dude, and the date would come sooner rather than later.

However, her family would be present and in support of the entire event and relationship. Her mother would probably beat her to the church and push her down the aisle if she needed it, but there was no pushing needed for Ava. Kevin was the love of her life, and she had never felt like this before. She cherished every moment with him and hoped for the day she would become his wife. She would cherish that moment above all, as Ava welcomed the feelings of true love and all the benefits it would offer her heart and life.

Happy to change into her flats for the reception, Ava soon found Kevin, Toni, and Eric at their designated table. They sat to the side of the bride and groom's table. Each table setting was adorned with white linen tablecloths and napkins with burgundy plates with a formal setting. Crimson and cream flowers that rested in glass bowl vases were the centerpieces. Lisa's brother played soft jazz, and people received their dinner plates from the servers.

Lisa and her new husband spent most of their money on the reception, so it would be a party and night to remember for the both of them. Every time someone hit their glass with their fork, the two joined in a lip lock. Each one was longer than the previous one. Yes, they were in love, whether her family supported the relationship or not. That could be seen in the details of the décor and the look in their eyes as they gazed at one another.

Ava sat down as Kevin pulled out her chair. "Hey, guys. Glad you all could make it. I know Lisa appreciates it."

Kevin kissed Ava's cheek. "No problem, babe. Anywhere you are, that's where I want to be."

Toni's grin grew into an all-out cheese. "How sweet, Kevin."

"Yeah, man. Hold that down." Eric caressed Toni's shoulder. "You making me look bad."

They all shared a laugh then started in on their main courses. Ava, elated to have Lisa's guests taste her creations, was proud to have given Lisa a discount. As her funds for the wedding festivities were low, Ava saw it as an occasion to give back as well as to try new sauces that she had been putting together. So far, no complaints.

After Kevin completed the prayer over the meal, Ava immediately cut into her chicken. "So how have you been, Toni, girl? I've missed you."

"I've been just great. I've been modeling here and there, but most of all just enjoying married life. It's better the second time around. Even though he is getting to be ol' school." Toni let out a hearty laugh.

Eric chuckled. "Stop it now. You know you love it."

"Well, you are. And yes, I do love it." Toni's and Eric's lips touched. "He's about to be thirty-five." Toni snapped her fingers. "Oh, and you two don't forget that I'm having a birthday dinner for him, so keep the seventh of March open on your calendar."

"Will do. This is just great." Ava applauded. "You two seem very happy."

"That we are, Ms. Ava," Eric chimed in. "I love my Toni and am so grateful God restored my marriage."

Ava was glad her mother was not in attendance to slide in a comment about marriage. Her mother was never short on words, especially when it came to relationships and marriage, mainly Ava's lack of being married. Ava knew she wanted the best for her, but she could be over the top at times when stating her thoughts. Every time Ava brought a boyfriend to meet her parents, it never turned out well. There was always the lingering question

Ava's mother would add to any conversation: "Will there be wedding bells in the future?"

Kevin took another bite of his glazed chicken, staying silent. Did he have nothing to add, or was he avoiding any talk about marriage? Ava didn't want to analyze the situation too much. He was there by her side, and he had been there for a little over six months. She'd broken her record of the five months she'd spent with Xavier. Ava just needed to sit back and enjoy the courtship and the growth that took place in their friendship and relationship as a whole. He was her best friend, and things were good. She needed to stop analyzing every little thing about their relationship and just be appreciative of the love they shared for one another.

Kevin wiped his mouth with his white linen napkin and then turned to her with those beautiful, inviting brown eyes. "You want to dance, babe?"

That was still one of her favorite questions to answer. She felt wanted and special. However, she secretly longed for the day she would have her first dance with her husband. Well, this wedding was the perfect stage for her to pretend. Ava indulged in the dream but didn't want to stay too long and go too wild with her imagination. She definitely didn't want to set herself up for hurt and disappointment.

After a few songs played and Ava and Kevin got to jam to an upbeat groove and semi-grind to a slow tune as well, it was time for the best man and maid of honor toasts. Nervous about what she would say, since her and Lisa's relationship wasn't one that was close, she allowed the best man to go first. While he spoke, she replayed in her head what she would want to hear on her wedding day.

When it was her turn, she stood, saying a quick prayer in her head to let the words flow with confidence. Looking at the happy couple, Ava said, "I wish Lisa and Matthew the absolute very best. I pray the love they share will guide them through the highs and lows of life. May they forever remember this day as the day they joined as one, and move forward in their bond that no one can break." She tilted her head and smiled toward the newlyweds. "May you two always support each other's dreams and all you wish to become, and live boldly, love unconditionally, and laugh often."

Kevin grabbed her hand. She lifted her glass of champagne as he lifted his water glass. "Everyone please join me in toasting this beautiful couple."

Ava made it through her toast. Could anyone tell by her words that she didn't know Lisa that well? She didn't give any personal anecdotes, but her words were sincere and, hopefully, they'd stick and be true for her one day as well. Would that day ever truly come for her, though? Was Kevin even headed in that direction? Or would his mother try to change his course?

Stop with the analysis. Just enjoy. Those words were definitely easier said than done. Since Ava wanted to be married more than anything else, not looking at her situation too closely would be a difficult task. She'd have to pray her way through and believe her dream would come true. But was her dream God's will for her life? If her desire and God's will were not the same, which one did she desire more? Only time would tell.

However, at thirty-one of age, she was running out of time. With Toni and Eric's elation on her right and Lisa and Matthew's happiness to the left, Ava wanted her day to come much sooner rather than later. Kevin needed to get on the fast track. They were perfect for each other. She knew it. He had to know it too. Ava just needed him to show he knew it by putting a ring on her finger. Then all would be well. At least in her eyes.

Chapter Fourteen

As the festivities slowed down at the reception, Ava and Kevin returned to their table to find Toni and Eric in a heated discussion. What had happened during the few minutes they were on the dance floor? When she and Kevin left, they were all lovey-dovey, acting as if they couldn't keep their hands off of one another. The tide had definitely changed suddenly.

"I can't believe you, Eric." Toni pushed his shoulder then looked away from him.

"What? I didn't do anything. She came up to me. I didn't invite her over here. Was I supposed to be rude?" Eric seemed embarrassed to be called out in front of the others at the table.

Ava could tell in words and body language that the happy couple had transformed into something very unhappy. Should she and Kevin go back out on the floor or go mingle, so they could have their privacy?

"Ava." *Too late.* Toni had just invited her into the conversation. "If someone comes up to you and starts talking to you, and you know they're trying to holla, what is the appropriate amount of time before you let them know you are with someone?"

Looking into Eric's eyes filled with shame and Toni's face filled with anger, Ava raised her hands and said, "Uh, as soon as possible?" Was speaking the truth wrong? Would she be the cause of this fight?

"Thank you." Toni slapped the table. "Case closed."

Ava didn't want to close any cases. She just wanted to have a good time at the reception, and it seemed her good time was about to be threatened. She knew to do her best to stay out of couples' spats. Of course, she would side with her girl. Ava couldn't ignore the girl code, but she wanted to appear neutral, especially in public. Hopefully, that tactic would help to keep things calm.

Just then, Kevin's phone went off. "Hold on, Ava. It's my mom. I'm gonna take this. Excuse me." He stood and walked out the side door out of the banquet hall.

Yep, her good time was about to go right out the window. *He sure hopped up quick.* What was it this time that he had to jump up to take her call so quickly? *Enough comparing.* Didn't matter anyway. Gladys was his mother, but Ava was his woman, and Ava was sure he knew and appreciated the difference. So what if he ran to his mother's aid at the speed of light? As long as he answered to Ava, she was good. *Right?*

Her past included guys who played the role of being interested then ignored her phone calls days after, sending mixed signals. Ava never understood why it was so hard for most men to communicate. Either they wanted the relationship or they didn't. All they had to do was let her in on it. Kevin was nowhere near the level of her past fools. He was gigantic steps above the mistakes of her past, yet she appreciated what she learned from each of them. Kevin would be able to reap the benefits of Ava's lessons learned.

Toni stood and grabbed her purse off the chair. "Ava, I'm sorry, but we're gonna head out. Not feeling this scene anymore, and I don't want to act out of my nature."

"Are you sure?" Ava nibbled at the leftover lettuce from her salad.

"Yes, girl. Be sure to thank Lisa for the invite and wish her my very best." Toni seemed to be in a rush as she turned to Eric. "I'ma run to the restroom and then we can be on our way."

Ava stepped toward her to give her a hug. As she came out of the embrace, Eric picked up Toni's jacket from the chair to assist her with putting it back on. Toni snatched the jacket out of his hand and walked out. Eric, seemingly ashamed, followed as Toni hustled to the bathroom located at the exit of the reception hall.

Sitting at the table alone, Ava reflected on her situation. Every relationship had its own struggles, but would she and Kevin ever have it out over him talking to another female? He did it every day, especially at work and in his counseling sessions. In fact, Glory was one of his closest friends. That's how she and Ava became so close, through his friendship with her. Ava would do her best to not make the "women as friends" thing their issue. She had enough to deal with in Kevin's family. She would keep her own golden rule intact: trust the man in her life until he gave her a reason not to. Ava couldn't make any promises, but she would do her absolute best.

Just at that time, Kevin returned to the table. "Hey, baby."

"What's up?" She was glad to lay her eyes on his handsome frame again. He cleaned up very well, and it did her heart some good.

"Nothing. Just my sister Martha asking my mom where I'm at and was I still planning to go to my nephew's sports banquet."

Ava sat back in her chair. "And?"

He leaned in close to her. "I told her I made plans with you."

"And?" She folded her arms. Ava was thankful for his response to her, but she knew his sister wouldn't let the situation go away that quietly. There was always something more to it.

"And she wasn't happy, but she'll have to get over it." He caressed Ava's shoulder.

Proud that he supported his girlfriend in this circumstance, she threw a little more respect his way. However, now his mother would be sure to blame her for his absence. Ava needed to discuss the very large elephant that sat at their table with them. "I appreciate you staying with me. This time. But I don't want your family resenting me if you're missing family events to be with me."

"Ava, it will always be something. I'd rather just stay here." He almost sounded like a whiny child, and she couldn't take that right then.

"Listen, why don't we just leave here and go there? Lisa will understand." Ava wiped her mouth with her napkin. "Really, us being here is not that serious. We've been here a good minute anyway."

He glared down at the table. "Well, that's what I suggested."

"And?" She added a sweeter tone to the question this time.

"Martha wanted me to come alone." Kevin grabbed a tight hold of Ava's hand as if he would need to calm her down from the news. "So I said I wasn't going to come at all."

Heat rose in her stomach. What was his sister trying to prove? "Again, I appreciate that, but they already don't like me for some reason or another, and I don't want to add fuel to their fire."

"They don't like you?" He bent his head and rubbed her hand. "What makes you think that, babe?" His eyes grew sad. Knowing Kevin, he probably wanted to shield Ava from the pain of being ostracized by his family, but she already felt it twenty times over. Would God forgive him for knowing the truth? His family didn't like anyone he brought home; maybe that was why he stayed away from love. The relationship would always be plagued by his family's behavior and words.

"They weren't very nice to me at your mother's birthday party, and that's fine, but I haven't done anything that I know of to offend them or cause them to dislike me." *And if I did, they could be grown about it and say something instead of acting like the mean girls in high school.* "So I'm not sure how to respond or act toward them at this point. However, I also don't want you missing a special night for your nephew. He deserves to have his uncle present."

"You are so sweet, Ava. I thank you for thinking of my nephew, but please know that my older sisters have always been overprotective, and it's not just you they've treated like that." He stared into her eyes as he continued to caress her hand. "And I've talked to them before about their behavior. If they choose to continue to act that way, they'll see less and less of me, because I want to be with you, and to have me there is to have you there too."

Could Ava marry Kevin right then and there? "Thank you, Kev. I'm glad you feel that way. I couldn't ask for anything better from you, but I don't want you to miss out on this because your sister is acting a certain way. It's not fair to your nephew." She chose her words carefully when describing his sister's behavior. Yes, he sided with Ava, but that didn't mean he couldn't change if she disrespected his family. She would be who she was and not allow their behavior to affect hers. She wouldn't stoop to their level.

Kevin drummed his fingers on the table, seeming to be deep in thought, as if he was waiting for her approval again. How could Ava deny being there for his nephew?

Did he think she was the kind of person who didn't care for others?

Ava placed her hand on top of his. "I'm serious. Go. I don't even know this chick that well. No need for you to stay. Toni can drop me off on her way home. She went to the restroom and then they're leaving. I can probably catch her and roll with them."

"Are you sure? I mean, yes, it would be nice to see my nephew get his award, but I don't want to leave you hanging . . . again." He ran his fingers through her hair.

"Really, it's okay, Kevin. Go. Don't worry about me. I'll be just fine."

It was okay to a certain extent. He had said all the right things, and Ava really didn't want Kevin missing out on family stuff because of his sister's immaturity, but they would have to be put in check, either by Kevin or by Ava. It didn't really matter to her by whom, but she knew it would have to be done, because there had to be some respect across the board. Could Ava be asking too much? Would Kevin retreat at the mention of his family's untimely request?

Chapter Fifteen

Ava couldn't wait to see Kevin again. As she drove to his house, she anticipated feeling the warmth of his arms around her as she prayed for them individually and as a couple. Only God knew what was to be, but as they continued to foster their relationship and do their best to keep Him at the center of it, hopefully all would turn out how she hoped and always dreamt.

Headed to his church that morning, she knew worshipping with him would draw her closer to Kevin every time she saw him. A lot of different things were attractive to her about him, but seeing him raise his hands in worship to the Father was at the top of the list. Plus, seeing him in his three-piece suit, clean cut and smelling good, didn't hurt the attraction factor one bit.

When she pulled up in his driveway, she saw a familiar car but couldn't place where she'd seen it before. Fear of the unknown crept in, but Ava wasn't going to let anything keep her from getting into the arms of her man.

Before she could knock on the door, Kevin pulled the door back and greeted her with his welcoming demeanor. She leapt into his arms. The hold from him was worth the wait. Ava could stay there for the rest of her life—and she wanted to.

"Hello, Ava." His mother's voice halted her feelings of forever.

Ava stepped back out of his hug as if she were a little girl getting caught in an act of something she wasn't supposed to be doing. "Hi, Ms. Allen. Hope all is well with you."

"You can call me Gladys."

She smiled. "Hi, Gladys." Was this the first of good things to come?

His mother opened her arms toward Ava for an embrace of her own. What was she up to? *Kevin must've had that much-needed talk with her. Don't analyze. Just go with it. Be thankful.*

Ava caught Kevin taking in the show of affection. Seeing him happy made her happy. She'd do her part to make the relationship with his mother work, but that's all she could promise. Gladys needed to meet her halfway. Or at least a third of the way.

"So, Ava, how have you been?" His mother took a seat on the arm of the loveseat.

"I've been wonderful, and you?" Ava carefully walked around the glass and wood coffee table and sat down on the plastic-covered flower-print sofa.

"Things are going okay." Gladys crossed her legs. "Thought I'd go to church with my son today. Is that okay with you?"

"Of course. I'd like that." *As long as you keep playing nice.*

"Well, that's good to know, especially since you tried to keep him from going to his nephew's banquet last night."

Kevin threw his hand up. "Momma, don't start. We just talked about this."

"I'm grown, Kevin. Remember, you came out of me and not the other way around. I can say what I want to anyone that spends time with you. I have to make sure they're with you for the right reasons. Understood?" she snapped at him.

As heat enveloped her body, Ava thought of the right words to say next. Her words needed to be direct but not disrespectful. *Her* parents taught her better than that. "I didn't keep him from anything. In fact, I'm the one who suggested he leave the wedding and go to the banquet. I didn't want him to miss his nephew's big day."

"Oh, is that so?" She rolled her neck. "Martha told me a different story."

Already tired of the conversation, Ava rolled her eyes. Playing nice was over. "You can believe what you want, but that's the truth. How would Martha know anyway? She wasn't even there."

Kevin hung his head. "Very true."

"So you're taking her side, Kevin?" Gladys stood and placed her hand on her hip. "This is not accepted. I don't think Ava will be here much longer anyway, so say what you must to play to her."

"Momma, there are no sides. There's only what's right and what's wrong, and right now, you're wrong. I can't believe you, Momma. We just spoke about this. I told you accepting Ava is accepting a new part of me."

"Excuse me." She peered at Ava and shook her head. "See, this disrespect from my son is because of you. He's never talked to me like this. Never. What are you putting into his mind?"

Ava shrugged her shoulders. She'd had enough. It was time she put her foot down if Kevin wasn't going to. "He's a grown man. I don't control him. He can say and do whatever he wants, including telling you his mind."

"Well, I'm glad to hear that. I know you tried to control the last man you were with by getting pregnant, and when that didn't work out, you latched onto my son, taking his kindness for weakness. What do you intend to do this time? The same as you did to your last?"

Kevin raised his voice as he walked toward her. "Momma! That's enough. You have to stop this."

Ava shook her hand at him. "It's okay, Kevin. I can handle ignorance. It's not a problem for me at all."

His mother stood and walked in Ava's direction. "Ignorance? Excuse me, missy. You better watch who you call ignorant, before I teach you about ignorance."

Ava put her hands on her hips. "So you get to say whatever you want and I can't defend myself." She placed her hand on Kevin's chest. "I need to get out of here. This is just too much for me."

"Yeah, you do that." Gladys clapped. "First good news of the day. The Lord has answered my prayer. This wench is nothing but trouble and needs to be cast out of your life permanently before she brings you down the wrong path like so many others in her life. I don't know if I could have forgiven you if I were a friend of yours. Only God can help you."

Ava looked back at her then grabbed her purse and headed out the door. She was hurt and discouraged by his mother's words. Where did she hear all that from? Was Kevin that oblivious to disclose all of her business to his mother? What was he thinking? Or was he even thinking?

Kevin followed her. "Ava, wait. I—"

Ava turned around just before she reached her car. "For what? To let your mother continue with her words tainted with judgment and spite? Over something she knows nothing about? Not me. Not today. Or did you tell her everything?"

"I'm sorry, but I did, because I am very serious about you, and I have never lied to my mother." He held his head down, knowing he took some part in his mother's behavior.

"Kevin, how could you? That was not something I would have told her about me so early on. Why not speak of the good qualities in me? The way I make you feel?

How happy we are when we're together? Did you decide that was too easy, or did you want to get rid of me from the start?"

"I never want to get rid of you, Ava. I just thought by being honest with my mother it would get her to see the good in you and forgive you for your past as God has." Kevin tried to bring her into his arms, but she pushed him away. He understood.

"I don't know how to feel about that, Kevin. This was not what I expected for a Sunday morning."

"Can we still go to church and pray about it together? I'm sure we will see it in a different light. Please say yes." He grabbed for her hand.

She quickly drew her hand back before he could touch it. "I am going to church. To my church, where at least if someone's judging me, they don't voice it out loud." Ava paused and looked into his eyes. "You know, your mother has some deep feelings about how we came together, and that's fine, but she will not disrespect me or accuse me of something that just didn't happen and she misconstrued in her mind."

Kevin stayed on Ava's heels as she opened her car door. "Please stay so we can talk about this. I want you to. We can get through this."

"I'm sorry, babe, but I'm all talked out. Especially with her. She doesn't know me or what I was going through when you and I met. God's forgiven me, and I have forgiven myself. She has nothing to do with my past, and if she keeps it up, she'll have nothing to do with my future either." Ava opened the car door wider and slid inside.

He placed his hands on the car door as if to try to stop her from pulling out of the driveway. "What's that supposed to mean?"

"I love you, Kevin—"

"And I love you, Ava."

She hit the electronic button to roll the window down as she closed the door. "I know you love me, and God knows I've been waiting for someone like you for my entire life, but I can't be with someone whose family is just plain nasty to me. That's just not fair to me. At least give me a chance before you judge me by my past mistakes."

He tapped the side of the car and looked to the sky, seeming to search for the right words to say. "I've told them. And I haven't let them get away with it either, every time."

"Yes, but it keeps happening, so they aren't respecting you or me." She hit the steering wheel. "I'm going to church. I will take this situation to the altar and try to leave it there. I suggest you do the same."

"I definitely will, for sure."

"Good, because you have a decision to make. You can choose a wonderful life with me, or choose your sisters' and mother's hateful attitudes, and miss out on someone who loves you and would show you that every day for the rest of your life." Ava wasn't thinking everything through. Her feelings were hurt, and to her it seemed as if he didn't care to fix it.

"Ava, you can't make me choose between you and my family. That's not fair."

"I'm just telling you how I feel. I can't keep going around them, stepping on eggshells and feeling uncomfortable. That's not how I want to live the rest of my life. I don't want to fight for your love or attention."

"I understand, but—"

The front door of the house swung open, and Gladys poked her head outside. "We better leave, Kev. We're going to be late for church."

Ava laughed then said, with a hint of sarcasm, "Looks like you gotta go. You have a blessed day, and I'll talk to you later."

The situation with Kevin's family wasn't at all what Ava had signed up for. As she drove back across town to her side of Houston and her church, she prayed for wisdom and discernment. "God, surely you wouldn't dangle Kevin in front of me only to take him away. He's my dangling carrot, and the rabbit never learns, does she?"

She'd give him some time to decide what he wanted to do. Ava promised herself that she wouldn't call or text him. He could see what his life was like without her in it. Even though they hadn't indulged in anything physical yet, he could enjoy the company of his family and see how that kept him warm at night.

The only problem with that was, who would keep Ava warm at night?

Chapter Sixteen

Three days had gone by and still not a word from Kevin. Was he trying to drive Ava crazy? They'd talked almost every day since the very beginning of their relationship. She missed their deep, meaningful, and funny conversations. She missed his voice. She missed him.

When Ava felt herself heading into a depressed state, she cooked. Taking a drive to the grocery store would hopefully prove to be beneficial. She could clear her head and get out of the house for a bit. She made sure to throw her cell phone in her purse. For the past few days, it had been attached to her hip so she wouldn't miss the call she'd been waiting for. Staring at anything that long would drive even the sanest person insane.

As she was en route to the store, she thought about what the perfect meal would entail. What would she cook for Kevin if he needed a pick-me-up? Seasoned grilled chicken would be involved, as that bird was a favorite for them both. Some green beans and macaroni and cheese, with a nice, modest salad, would round out the menu. She'd be sure to get the fresh green beans and create her famous concoction that she was known for. The seasoning and herbs blend she created always had folks coming back for a second helping.

Seeing couples in the store holding hands, deciding on what cereal to buy, or having a small disagreement, all enhanced her feelings of missing Kevin. Should she call him just to say hi and see how he was doing? *No. Stay strong. He should call you. He's the one with the crazy family. He's the one who was wrong by not standing up to his mother.*

Ava made her way through the produce section, choosing the best-looking and freshest ingredients for her perfect salad. As she mulled over the green beans, she felt someone's eyes on her. She slowly turned around to see if she was just imagining it, not wanting to look silly if she was. Could it be Kevin?

"Hello, beautiful lady. I thought that was you." Xavier, her ex-boyfriend, stood in the middle of the aisle between the watermelon and cantaloupes looking as handsome as ever. *Sweet.*

She tried to keep herself from jumping back but wasn't that successful. "Well, hi, X. You startled me. What a surprise, bumping into you here. You were never the cooking type."

"Am I that scary? Yes, this is true. Oh, how I miss your meals."

He had been scary in the past, but she didn't know what he was on that day. However, she didn't want to bring up old stuff. "Not scary at all. How have you been?"

"I've been pretty good." Xavier stepped back and looked her up and down. "Looks like you're doing great. You look wonderful; not that you didn't look as wonderful before."

Glad she had lost that fifty pounds since she last saw him, she knew he would see a difference, especially since he seemed to obsess over her weight more than she did when they were together. "Well, thank you. You know, eating well and getting some exercise in."

"Well, it's agreeing with you. But I should be thanking you."

Not sure what to think of his words, Ava dove in. "What do you mean by that? There's nothing to thank me about."

"You helped me realize the way I treated you wasn't right. Honestly, I didn't want to ever hurt you, Ava. I hope one day you will be able to believe that and forgive me for my behavior."

"Mmm." She pursed her lips.

"I mean it." He rubbed the back of his head. "I was horrible to you. You are a beautiful woman, inside and out, and I took that for granted. I wish I could go back and treat you how you deserve to be treated. I just wish I had a second chance."

"Well, Xavier, I appreciate that. I really do."

"Yeah, and I've started going back to church recently. I'm trying to become a better man in every area of my life. I gave my life to God for Him to show me the right way. I wanted to call you and let you know, but I didn't think you would answer my call."

Who is this guy and where was he during the course of our relationship? Was he there all along and all I had to do was take him to church?

He looked down at his hands and then took a deep breath. "I hate to be too forward, but are you seeing anybody?"

Ava, for the first time in months, didn't know how to answer that question. "Well . . . yeah."

Xavier chuckled. "Are you sure? That doesn't sound so confident. I don't want to make you feel that you have to say yes."

She smiled. "No, not at all. And yes, I'm sure."

On that day, at that time, she believed she still had a boyfriend but couldn't be sure, and with Xavier saying all the right things and looking the way he did, she needed to tread lightly. All he had taken her through while they were together had done a number on her self-esteem. Yes, he may have changed, but how long would that last? Deep down she knew he wasn't for her, but for the next chick in line. She was in love with Kevin, and she took the encounter as a test from God. There was no temptation to persuade Ava.

"Would it still be all right to take you out sometime? As a thank you, of course."

She contemplated a few seconds too long, and then said, "No, that probably wouldn't be a good idea. I'm glad you are making positive changes though. I always felt you had it in you."

"It's because of you, Ava." He moved a little closer to her. "Are you sure you can't give me another chance? I want marriage, kids, the whole nine. I see that now, and I feel like I'm seeing you here for a reason, so I gotta ask."

"Xavier, like I said, I'm glad you have made positive changes, but I am with somebody, and I am in love with him. I'm happy for you and wish you the best, but that's all I can do."

"I respect that." He gave her a hug. "Just know that knowing you has changed my life. Never forget that." Xavier winked and walked off.

The timing of everything in her life was all messed up. Xavier's family had always welcomed her into their family and home. Could she play God just for a second and put Kevin in Xavier's family? She knew that was too much to ask, but that would be the perfect scenario.

After paying for her items at the checkout, she bounced back to her car with a little more pep in her step than before. If she could have that effect on hardheaded Xavier, what could happen with her and Kevin, the man of her dreams? He had to be it.

Her phone buzzed as the special ring tone of Jagged Edge's "I Gotta Be" played, and Kevin's picture appeared on the screen. *Finally*. Ava was about to receive favor for turning down Xavier's date proposal. She was strong enough to say no to him, and she got the call she had been waiting for. Funny how things worked like that.

"Hey, Ava. Do you have a minute?"

For you, I have a lifetime. "Yes." She quickly loaded her three bags in the car and took a seat behind the wheel.

"I just wanted to talk to you for a minute. I won't be long."

"I'm listening." *Take your time. I've been waiting for this apology.*

"Well, I know my family can be a bit much to take in, but they are my family, and if they see red flags, then I can't just ignore it."

"Okay, but you said so yourself that they give everyone a hard time. Like no woman would ever be good enough for you." Ava gauged how much attitude she included in that response. Did she need more? Less? Or maybe none at all.

"Yes, but this relationship seems more of a struggle than any other."

"It's not a struggle for us. It's a struggle for them. And I'm in love with you, not them."

"That's just it." He cleared his throat. "The woman I'm with, I want her to love me *and* my family. Even though it may be a bit rough at first, they are a part of me."

"Well, it's not my fault they see me as the enemy." More attitude released. She wanted to control her anger, but she wasn't about to let his family dictate her love life. Ava had waited long enough for the right man to show up, and now that he was here, she was going to put up a good fight, even if they were related to the witches of Eastwick.

"And I'm not saying it is, but I just need to take a step back from everything right now and look at what I really want."

What he really wants? Did all the time they shared together the past six months not clue him in on what he wanted? And now he wasn't sure? "So are you saying you don't love me anymore?" She was ready to jump through the phone. "Are you telling me that this is it, because your mother couldn't hold her judgment against me from the start? How can you do this to me? I love you, Kevin. I can't force myself on anyone. For some reason, your family just doesn't like me."

"Ava, that's not what I'm saying at all. I do love you. I just need some time to figure some things out. I have to do this. I'm sorry. I just hope you can understand."

"Well, don't bank on me waiting forever for you to figure things out. You're letting your family dictate our relationship, and that doesn't sit well with me at all."

"I know, but you gave me an ultimatum the other day, so I'm just taking everything into consideration. I can't fully go on without mulling everything over. I cannot choose, and the more you put me in the middle, my family will always come first. I'm sorr—"

"Fine. Good-bye." She needed to hang up before all the cuss words she knew flowed freely from her mouth. *Dang. What was Xavier's number? Shame on me for deleting his number from my phone. You don't mean that, girl. Oh, yes, I do!* This was not happening. The man she was supposed to spend the rest of her life with just put her on the back burner for an indefinite amount of time.

Ava sat in her car, stunned by the whole conversation. Was she not supposed to speak up about this situation? Wasn't her future at stake too?

What had just happened? A week ago she was in a relationship with the man she knew God had brought into her life to one day marry, and no one on this earth could've told her any different. Now, she was alone. Again. This pattern was beyond getting old. Ava didn't want much—a husband, a house, some children. Why was that dream so hard to obtain? As she started the car, she stared into space looking for answers, hoping the answer would fall right into her lap. Nothing ever came down but the heavy burden of the feelings of loneliness and the heavier weight of regret. She wanted to go back and withdraw her ultimatum, but now it was too late. She would be sure to choose her words more carefully in the future—if there was another chance. What had she done? She would do it another way, if only God would give her another chance.

Chapter Seventeen

Sunday morning, Ava found herself at the altar for a different reason. Instead of standing by a bride in support, she knelt, hands cupped together in sorrow. Soon, a prayer partner would meet her where she was and pray for her need. As she waited her turn, her mistake stared her in the face. What had she done? Kevin was the best man she'd ever been in a relationship with. She had let her emotions guide her words; and her words offered up an ultimatum to the godly man she believed the Lord had finally brought into her life. Why was she trying to mess that up? Why did she need all the attention? Was she not satisfied with what God had given her?

In movies and sad songs, people would always talk about not being able to breathe. Those lines and lyrics had always seemed a bit extreme—until now. As she gasped for air with her hand over her heart, she understood the concept all too well. She had to get out of that sanctuary before she had a breakdown in front of the entire church body to give them something else to talk about.

Just before she could stand, a middle-aged woman in a pants suit took hold of her hands. "What would you like to pray about?"

Ava shook her head. "Never mind. I'm okay." She braced herself on the post to stand up. The woman squeezing her arm stopped her movement.

"Well, I'm sure you came up here for a reason. Now let's pray about your situation and watch how God can turn it around."

As the lady spoke with eloquence and sincerity, she prayed words of hope and faith. Not wanting to share too many details, Ava knew that her Heavenly Father already knew the situation, and that was enough for her. It seemed to be enough for the prayer partner as well. She continued her encouraging words and threw in a few scripture verses. When Ava heard Jeremiah 29:11 come out of her mouth, she began to tear up. She rested in the fact that God had a plan for her life, a plan for her good. The Lord supplied the perfect scripture at the right time.

She didn't need to worry about anything; however, she wasn't sure what to do with the pain of missing Kevin's touch, his face, and his heart. After the prayer and hugs were exchanged, Ava still felt like leaving. If she couldn't be with Kevin, she didn't want to be around anyone.

When she arrived at her car, she thought of how she and Kevin would travel to church together and he would always be sure to beat her to the car door to open it for her. It had been a while since she had to open her own door in that parking lot. Those thoughts restarted her tears as they seemed to jump out of her eyes.

Ava did her best to make it home safely without having her tears temporarily blind her vision. Constantly wiping her eyes and cheeks made it hard to see and navigate through the streets. God needed to steer her home. He needed to take the wheel in more than one area of her life.

As soon as she walked into the house, she took off her blouse, changed into her pajama top and thick sleep socks, and then crawled into bed. She had never hyperventilated before but believed she was currently going through it. Her chest vibrated as she gasped for air anywhere she could get it. The pain was unreal. Could Ava just stop feeling for a minute? Or, better yet, go back to the time before she fell in love with Kevin? If only she had some sort of time machine. She would go back and change it all. First she would have never made the mistake of sleeping with her best friend's fiancé. Now that she thought about it, that would be the only thing she would change. It was the start of her entire downward spiral.

The past couple of days were some of the hardest she had ever lived. Praying at the altar gave her some peace, but all she could do was think about Kevin. His smile, his laugh, their first meeting, first kiss, and how he had accepted her from the beginning for the person she was and not what she looked like physically. He never said a word about her being a plus-sized woman and had always downplayed her insecurities and made her feel beautiful. She appreciated that more than anything. Now was that gone too?

Lying in bed with those thoughts running through her head couldn't be good for her mind; but it was easier to just give in. Give it all up. Forget it all. Ava wanted to be married, and Kevin resembled the real deal. She now grieved the fact that she may have lost out on her dream becoming a reality with him. He was the perfect man for her, and there would be no other like him.

Her stomach growled. *When was the last time I ate?* For the first time in a long time, maybe forever, Ava couldn't remember when she had last eaten. She hadn't eaten that morning or at all the day before. Could that really be true? She of all people had never missed a meal. If Kevin had been with her, he'd have scolded her for that last thought. Ava needed him in her life. It would have been nice to hear from him right in that moment. Should she call him? She could just check on him and see how he was doing. They didn't have to talk long. Just to see if he was doing okay.

Before she knew it, she had her cell phone in hand and was scrolling through the numbers on her phone. She called Kevin, and with each ring, her heart jumped in her throat. She couldn't wait to hear his voice and anticipated being able to hear in his tone that he missed her.

When his voice mail came on, her spirit fell. It was disappointing to say the least. Hearing his deep tone on the opposite end of the phone would've done her heart some good. What was he doing and who was he with where he couldn't answer his phone? Or even worse, did he look at the screen and see it was her calling and simply put the phone back down? Did he find another so quickly? Nausea set in as her stomach ached. What was going on with her? She hadn't expected to fall that hard or that quickly for him, or anyone else, for that matter, but Ava truly cared for him and loved him dearly, and she wanted the love of her life back. Ava needed him back.

The idea of going over to his house crossed her mind, but she didn't want to seem like a crazy stalker. If she came off as an insane, needy woman, he may be turned off, and the whole scene could push him further away from her than he already was.

She hadn't had a drink since that horrible night she betrayed her and Rene's friendship. Drinking got her nowhere but in trouble. After her fourth glass of wine or so that night, Rene's fiancé at the time, Ishmael, could have said anything and she would've jumped into bed with him. She didn't even recall what he did say, but she did remember the happenings between the sheets and the pain it caused her friend. The two ladies' friendship did recover, though, after an accident almost caused her to lose her life.

Rene found it in her heart to forgive Ava after what Ishmael had done. What man would have no remorse killing their unborn child and nearly killing Ava? Ava slowed down her alcohol intake since that night ended in very poor judgment on her part. Since Kevin was a recovering addict and no longer consumed alcohol, she put the alcohol down for more than one reason, a "two birds with one stone" sort of thing. However, she needed a drink now.

She should've stopped on the way home to grab a bottle of wine. There was that bottle of champagne she'd been holding on to for a special occasion. This was an occasion, but she didn't know how special it was. In fact, it was just the opposite. She'd toast to how stupid she felt. If she got a good enough buzz going, she may even feel like eating. Her situation was beyond sad, as Ava now needed to trick herself to eat. Drinking would make her numb to her reality of being alone.

Sitting on her porch, glass in hand and thoughts whirling around in her brain, she imagined Kevin pulling into the parking lot. He'd then run up to her third-floor apartment, hold her in his arms, and tell her how much he loved her and how he would never let go again.

In the past months they were together, he'd shown her what it was like to be treated like a prized possession. How could she give him an ultimatum because his family was rude? She could have handled it another way. Couldn't she? One had nothing to do with the other. She didn't have to have a good relationship with them to have a great relationship with him. If only she could go back.

After finishing three glasses, she threw together a turkey and cheese sandwich. That was the best she could do. She had no energy to create a full meal. Her love for cooking had subsided, among other things.

She chewed her food, but it didn't taste the same. The taste made her sick. Ava wanted to call Kevin again, hoping he'd pick up this time. Thirty minutes had passed by. Maybe he was free now. Ava just wanted some hope. She dialed his number again.

"Hello?" He seemed less than thrilled to answer the phone.

"Hey, babe." She expressed enough excitement for the both of them. "I just wanted to tell you how much I miss you, Kev."

"Well, thank you."

Is that it? "So have you missed me at all?"

He cleared his throat. "Of course, but I'm trying to keep my head space free. I've been thinking about you and hope you're doing well."

"I'm not. All I do is think of you." She fought back her tears. "Can we have lunch or something? Talk some things out? Even just coffee."

"Not sure that'd be a good idea. There is still a lot I have to work out on my own, Ava."

"Well, I just want to apologize for painting you into a corner. I didn't mean it like that. I was just hurt. I felt like your family was ganging up on me without even giving me a chance. From the moment I met your mother, she didn't like me." Of course, now, though, the pain of him not wanting to be in a relationship with her was more excruciating. She was pleading her case the best she could after three glasses of champagne.

"I understand, and I appreciate your apology, but I need more time. And right now, we can't find Tweet. That's my main concern at this time."

"I thought she was staying at the rehab facility." She was smiling for all the wrong reasons. He let her in on a family thing, and that made her elated. It made her feel included again.

"We did too." Kevin smacked his lips. "But she snuck off the property a couple of days ago, and we haven't heard from her since."

"I'm sorry, babe. I hope you all find her soon."

"Thank you, Ava. I'll talk with you later." He hung up the phone without another word.

The sadness in his voice only drew her closer to him. She wanted to be there for him and his family. Well, for him and Tweet; not so much for the rest of his family. Ava wanted to hold him in her arms and tell him everything would be okay. At least he admitted he did miss her; yet he wasn't interested in seeing her or talking to her anymore. Her feelings were hurt. Hearing him say her name was worth it though. When she heard her name flow off the tip of his tongue, she felt special again. Worth something. She had missed that feeling.

Ava took a sip from her fourth glass of champagne. She was about to polish off the bottle when her stomach started to rumble. Something wasn't right. She made a dash to the restroom.

After losing her lunch and most of the champagne she had just consumed to the Tidy Bowl man, she sat on the floor and leaned back against the cabinet. She thought she had been in love with Xavier, but she never experienced pain like she was going through in that moment. The physical sickness was new to her. Her emotional torment was at the highest level it had ever been in her life. Kevin was perfect for her, and she had messed it up. Why did she keep messing up her life? It was on the perfect path, and if it weren't for her impatience with his family, she would be at his side trying to find Tweet.

"Lord, please take this pain away. This pain is like no other, and I honestly don't know what to do with it. I'm a tired, hot mess. I don't know what your plan is, but I need you. I need you to fix this." She took a deep breath and wiped her eyes. "And I need Kevin. Please help him realize that he needs me. I'm sorry for messing up what I believe you brought into my life for a reason. Help me to get out of my own way, Lord. Forgive me for having the feelings I do for his family. Give me understanding and strength to overcome what I have caused."

She rose up from the floor only to go jump back into the bed. She sent a text to her boss saying she wouldn't be in the next morning. All Ava could do was lie in bed and think of Kevin. She needed to do something different but didn't know what, so she stuck with what she did know to do. Pulling the covers over her head, she hoped the warm thoughts of Kevin would comfort her until she fell asleep. Hopefully, he'd show up in her dreams. At least they'd be able to be close for however long the dream lasted. At that point, Ava would take what she could get. All she wanted was for him to give her a second chance. Ava would do it differently. Instead of pushing him against a wall, she would take whatever his family dished out to her as long as he stood next to her for a lifetime.

Chapter Eighteen

The Saturday had arrived that Ava was to cater Eric's birthday party. After a week where she had only gotten out of bed to go the restroom and pick at food here and there, she had to make herself get up. She'd let her job know she had a serious stomach flu for two entire weeks, which was almost the truth. Her stomach, heart, and soul all suffered.

Nevertheless, Ava couldn't let a friend down. Toni had been looking forward to throwing Eric's birthday dinner for some time. She planned everything and wanted it to go off without a hitch. It was almost like she had a secret she couldn't wait to tell, even though he knew about it. She was a kid in a candy store, and Ava didn't want to put a damper on Toni's excitement for anything. Ava would have to put on her apron and a smile to get through the event.

Since she didn't feel like doing much, Ava called in some backup to get the meal complete and over to Toni and Eric's new house in time to set up everything. All she would need to do would be to reheat the stuffed grilled chicken balls and warm almond and strawberry salad. Ava would make it look presentable on the serving dishes and serve up her best. Rene, the extra help, was due at her apartment any minute.

As soon as Rene walked in to help bring the food over to Toni's, Ava hustled over to her to get a much-needed hug. She held on tight.

Rene rubbed her back, still in the embrace. "Are you okay, Ava?"

No matter how much she tried, Ava couldn't hold the tears in. "No, not at all."

"What's going on? Talk to me." She rubbed Ava's arm.

"I messed up, girl. Big time. I may have lost him forever."

Rene's puzzled look urged Ava to go ahead and tell her what was going on, as the last time they had a serious talk in her kitchen over food, it didn't end so well for her or Rene. An altercation would've occurred between the two behind the betrayal issues if Toni hadn't shown up in time to stop Rene from literally jumping all over Ava. Wanting to assure Rene the situation at hand had nothing to do with Rene or Paul, she went ahead to explain.

"Don't worry. It has nothing to do with you or Paul, girl. I learn from my mistakes."

"So why all the tears? Just come out and say it. You know it can't be that horrible." Rene guided her to take a seat.

"I just sort of made Kevin choose between me and his family. I messed up royally, and I don't know how to get him back."

"What?" Rene's look had settled from fear to confusion. "Why would you do that? What were you thinking?"

"I don't know." She shook her head as she snatched a few tissues out of the box on the nearby table. "Well, I know, but I didn't mean to take it that far. His mom and older sisters can be just plain mean, and I don't want them to dictate our relationship or put so many disgruntled feelings out there toward me to break us apart."

"So you decided to dictate it, huh?" Rene smiled.

"I know. It sounds so stupid." Ava knew Rene would call her out on her stuff. It was almost refreshing. Almost.

"I've been waiting for someone like him, and then I go and get in my own way and mess it all up. He broke things off, and I don't even think he will return now."

Rene needed something to distract her. She didn't want to make Ava feel even worse. She remembered Ava could go into the depths of sadness if you let her. Rene found some foil on the table and placed it over Ava's dishes. "Well, now just hold on. I know Kevin cares about you a lot. Maybe he just needs a little time, and then, I'm sure y'all will get back together."

"That's my hope, but I don't know. It doesn't look good, or sound good, for that matter." Ava's neck stiffened from holding it down so much.

Never making eye contact with Ava, Rene kept herself busy. "Have you talked to him lately?"

"I talked to him a couple weeks ago, but he kept it short." Ava placed the wrapped dishes in her catering bag. "And he was preoccupied with his little sister. He had to go out to search for her."

"Well, don't give up hope, Ava. Give him the space he needs, stay in prayer, and if y'all are supposed to be together, he'll come back to you. God wouldn't have it any other way."

"I know you're right, but that is easier said than done. All I think about is him. I haven't eaten much this week or gone to work." Ava placed the key lime pie in a covered pie pan.

"And you've been lying in your texts, too. I asked you how things were going, and you said fine."

"I didn't want to bother you." She also wanted to keep the embarrassment to a minimum.

"I'm your best friend. It's not a bother. Remember that. We've been through too much to lie to each other." Rene placed the last casserole dish in Ava's catering bag.

"I will." Ava could at least do that.

"Eric's birthday dinner will be a good distraction. Let's load up the car and roll out."

Ava finished wrapping up dishes and putting tops on Tupperware. After they made a few trips to the car, they were ready to head out.

After about a mile or so of only listening to the tunes on the radio, Ava finally wanted to replace thoughts of Kevin with something else. "So, Rene, what's new with you?"

"Oh, not much at all."

"Come on. We've been talking about me since you got to my place. How's everything going with Paul?" Ava's sincere interest had to be leaking out of her pores. She was so happy for her friend and wanted details.

Rene's lips tightened. "No, it's okay. I can tell you another time." She felt a bit awkward talking about her budding relationship while Ava was on the rocky side of hers.

"Are you kidding me? You got me curious now."

"Well . . ." Rene paused.

"What is it?" Ava turned down the radio.

"You might not want to hear this type of news, especially right now, since—"

Ava cut in immediately: "If it's good news, I need to hear it. And I'll be happy for you. You're my best friend. I want to celebrate with you, no matter what I'm going through." Ava placed her hand over her chest, then moved it to Rene's hand that rested on the armrest between them.

Rene sat silent, not knowing how to proceed. Should she leave out details? Should she make it seem that it was nothing spectacular?

Ava couldn't take it anymore. "Would you just spit it out, girl? And don't leave out anything."

"Okay." She put her hand up. "The other night at dinner, Paul began talking about our past and how we've known each other since high school and the only reason he hadn't asked me out sooner was because I was usually in a relationship."

"Mmm."

"And he went on about timing and how it's all according to God's plan anyway. Then he said he believed this was our time, and he wanted a future with me."

Ava's smile could probably be seen down the street. "Yes."

"He then took out this little velvet box, and my heart dang near jumped out of my body."

"Ooh, Rene." Ava's eyes squinted as her smile grew into full, all-out cheese. She tapped her fingers on the steering wheel in a celebratory clap for her friend's news. "I'm so happy for you!"

"He sweetly told me that he valued our friendship, cherished our relationship, and loved me more than anything. Then he asked me to marry him."

"Woo hoo! And you of course said . . . ?"

Rene tapped her leg. "Well, I said yes, but . . ."

"But what? Why is there always a but with you? Maybe because the lawyer is always in you." Ava's shoulders fell as she put the excitement on hold for a minute.

"I don't know, girl." Shaking her head, Rene continued to mess with her pant leg. She looked as if her nerves were running crazy on the inside. Was she nervous? Did she not want to be married?

"You don't know what, girl?" Confusion was at the forefront of Ava's mind. Rene seemed to be in a very favorable situation. Ava didn't understand what problem she had. He was a sweet, caring guy and went to church on a regular basis. What more did she want?

"It's complicated. I know Paul and I have been friends for a long time, and I truly do care about him. Even love him. I just think this is all happening too fast. Not to mention Ishmael keeps sending me letters from jail."

Ishmael, of course. "Not that it's any of my business, but what is he writing to you about?"

"You know, how much he's sorry. How he wants me to forgive him. He wants me to come see him. The usual sob story every man in jail has."

"Have you written him back?"

"Heck no. For what? So he can turn my life into misery again? No, thank you. I finally have the right man in my life and will not let Ishmael interject himself into it only to cause heartache and turmoil."

Ava went silent. She didn't want to rehash bad memories when everything was going so well for Rene.

"Ava, you know something?"

"What?" She now regretted asking about Ishmael.

Rene smiled at Ava. "I never thanked you for showing me how dirty Ishmael truly was. I was too caught up in the hurt and betrayal, but now I see it had to happen that way. I'm truly sorry that you lost your baby in all that happened, but again, maybe God planned it that way."

"Rene, there's no need for you to say any of those kind words. I'm the one who should be thanking you. You are a true friend to me, although you wanted to choke me out when you heard."

Rene laughed. "I couldn't get a hold of you because you had your guard dog Toni there."

Ava started to laugh with her. "Okay, enough of the dreaded past. Let's get back to the topic at hand. Now tell me why you're feeling like this about Paul."

"I just don't know. Everything is happening so fast. Yes, I have known him a very long time and, yes, he treats me like no man has ever come close to. I just don't know if I'm doing the right thing. I could be stepping into a 'feel good now, hurt later' type of thing. I just don't know."

"Does he make you happy? Does he bring a smile to your face when he's just in the room? Does he still give you butterflies in your stomach like a teenager?"

"Yes, yes, and yes." Rene was in full cheese mode.

"You have the right to move at your own pace, but believe me, you don't wanna let how you feel about one thing mess up something good. Ishmael will probably never get over you, but that's not your burden or emotion to carry. I think you and Paul are perfect for each other. Enjoy the relationship *and* planning the wedding."

"Well, that's it. Paul suggested we go to Jamaica and let the resort take care of everything. He recently got a big bonus at work and said he could fly out our family and close friends. All y'all would have to do is take care of your hotel accommodations." Rene's eyes lit up as she spoke. "And we could get a great group rate at the hotel where the wedding will take place. Even said there's a perfect spot on the beach to have the ceremony."

Ava was more than impressed with Paul's well thoughtout plans. "Seems like he's put a lot of thought into this."

"Yes, it's sweet, but a little nerve-racking."

Ava patted Rene's hand. "Let me assure you that Paul doesn't do anything he doesn't want to, and it seems like he really loves you. Your life with him would be what you have always deserved. Be happy and just go with it." *At least you're getting asked for your hand in marriage. I screwed up my chance.* "Let me see the ring."

Rene opened the inside pocket in her purse and pulled out a glowing half-carat princess-cut diamond that sat on top of a bling-encrusted band.

"Ah, Rene, that's beautiful." *Try not to get any drool on her ring.*

As Ava pulled into Toni and Eric's driveway, Rene carefully placed the ring in the inside zippered pocket of her purse. "I told Paul I'd put the ring on after the party, so don't say anything about it to Toni yet. I don't want to take away from their celebration."

Ava admired Rene's humility. She was sure that was one of the many qualities Paul loved about her. Howvere, even though this was a great step in Rene's life, Ava couldn't stop herself from hatin'. *Why can't it be me?*

True, Rene and Paul had known each other for a while, but they had only been romantically linked for a little while. Ava was a walking emotional contradiction. She was thrilled for Rene because she was her best friend and she did deserve every good thing that came her way, but Ava had been relationally challenged longer than Rene had, and waiting for her Mr. Right to propose to her. Rene now had three proposals under her belt, and Ava didn't even have one.

What was so special about Rene? What was lacking in Ava? Even after all the strides forward she had made in the last year or so emotionally, her insecurities never took long to resurface. She wanted only to focus on God's plan for her life, but with her and Kevin not together while everyone around her was getting married, "focus" wasn't the F word she wanted to use at that time. Could God do something with all the different emotions she experienced? Had He forgotten about her and her happiness? Did He even care? Was it just another test for her to pass before she got her prize? There were so many questions, and she needed all the answers.

Waiting for the one thing that would make her happy was now a recurring dream at this point. Her growing impatience was a lot to subdue. For now she would not think about what she didn't have, but the friends and love she did have. In all, Ava believed God would come through for her like He always had, in more ways than one.

Chapter Nineteen

Ava loved seeing the smile on Toni's face as she greeted them at the door, beaming with excitement. It had been a difficult road for her to get there. It was a path that had a lot of twists and turns, but the road seemed to be fixed and moving straight, even though they had a little hiccup at Ava's coworker's wedding.

Toni and Eric were another couple that were perfect for each other. They complemented one another well. Where Toni was weak, Eric was strong, and vice versa. Everyone in Ava's immediate circle had their soul mate by their side. There was Toni and Eric. Rene's Paul showed up with Ava's brother, Alex, and his wife. Even Glory and Greg, seemingly in good spirits, were in attendance for the birthday festivities.

Kevin was the only one MIA, which left Ava sitting there alone. She wanted to call and remind him about the dinner, hoping he'd come to support Toni and Eric, even if he didn't want to be around Ava at the moment. If he didn't answer, though, that would send her into an emotional frenzy, and she wanted to play it straight and just join in with Toni and Eric as they celebrated a special occasion in their lives. It shouldn't be about her. It was about Eric and Toni. She definitely didn't want it to turn into a pity party for her.

After getting all the food out on the buffet platters, Ava, Rene, and Toni did one last walk-through in the kitchen to make sure everything was in its place.

"Thank you two so much." Toni grabbed both of the ladies' hands as they stood in a mini circle next to the marble island.

Rene chuckled. "Mmm. Ava definitely gets all the credit on this one. She did all the cooking. All I did was help with the transporting."

Toni turned to Ava and gave her a tight squeeze. "Yes, thank you, ma'am. But I do thank both of you for being here. I wouldn't have it any other way."

"You're welcome. But where else would we be? He's special to you, and you're special to us." Ava set a casserole dish back on the island before she gave Toni another hug. She didn't need to have her hips knocking over anything, especially while they were having a moment.

"Let's break open one of those bottles early." Ava pointed to the group of Moët bottles that rested on the kitchen counter for the birthday toast. "We can toast to you and Eric." She craved a drink right about then.

Toni looked down. "I can drink water and toast with you guys."

Ava stared at her for about two seconds. "Ahh, I knew you were glowing for a reason. I just knew it!"

"Shh, Ava. I haven't told Eric yet. I'm going to surprise him later tonight for his birthday. Probably after we finish with dinner."

"Ooh." Ava covered her mouth. "Well, we can hold it. Can't we, Rene?"

"Of course." Rene grinned. "Well, for a little bit anyway."

They shared a group hug. "I'm so happy for you, girl." Ava, elated, grabbed a bottle of water out of the fridge and poured equal shares into three glasses. After giving one to each of her girlfriends, she then held up the third and said, "To Toni and Eric."

Rene repeated, "To Toni and Eric. They deserve the best."

Ava then leaned in and whispered, "And the little bun in the oven, my niece, who I will spoil." Ava giggled at the thought.

They giggled, clinking glasses. After they each took a sip, they returned to the living room where the appetizers were being served.

Ava wanted to catch up with Glory, so she found her first thing. "Hey, girl, it's been a while. How have you been?"

"Better." She mustered up a half smile.

"Well, that's good, right?"

Glory sighed and slowly swayed back and forth. "Yeah, it's good. But he still hasn't found a job, one that pays well anyway, and he's getting extremely frustrated. Not only taking it out on me, but now his anger is moving to the kids. It's up and down, but mostly down these days."

"Really? Greg?"

"Yep, I know. He's not himself though. The man he is now isn't the man I married. I know this is not the man I wanted to spend the rest of my life with. It scares me to think of what will happen between us." She twiddled her thumbs as if she was thinking about sharing more. "The kids and I went to stay at my sister's house for about a week. I think that scared him. Hopefully he saw how seriously his behavior affected us."

"That'll do it. I know he's been stressed out lately." Ava caressed Glory's shoulder. "But I know he doesn't want to lose you guys."

Glory huffed. "Hopefully, it was a wakeup call."

Greg approached them and put his hand around Glory's waist. He kissed her softly on the cheek and whispered something in her ear. She snickered and playfully rolled her eyes.

When it was time to sit down to dinner, everyone made their way to the table and sat next to their significant other. Since the rest of the grand dining table was full, no one noticed that Ava sat next to the only empty seat at the end of the table. Or maybe they did notice but just politely said nothing.

All the party guests devoured Ava's creations amid their conversations. Paul and Rene laughed together; then she kissed him and slid her engagement ring on her finger, looking him in the eyes. *She must've made peace with the yes she gave him to his marriage proposal.*

Eric lifted his fork, with a bite of his steak at the end of it, to Toni's mouth. She gladly ate it as she rubbed his shoulder. It was so sweet it was almost sickening. Ava didn't want to hate, but it couldn't be helped. Ava knew if Kevin had been there, they'd be displaying the same amount of affection toward one another, but that was just it. He wasn't there, and she was the reason. She had pushed him right on out of her life, and one of the consequences was attending functions on her own. She had hoped to be done with that season of her life, but it was beginning to look like she should just get used to it. There was no hope.

Although Glory and Greg were in a conversation about what seemed to be a more serious matter, they weren't arguing like they had been the last few times Ava spent time in their presence.

Glory shrugged her shoulders. "It's probably too short notice."

Greg threw his hands up and said, "Well, all you can do is ask them, right, Glory? The ladies can always say no."

Ava didn't mean to ear hustle, but her curiosity pushed her to speak up. "What's up, you two?"

"Nothing. Greg says I should ask you, Rene, and Toni if you'd like to come to our women's retreat next weekend."

Rene heard her name. "Tell me more."

Glory took a sip of her water. "It's next Friday through Sunday, and it's called Breathe: a Retreat for the Mind, Body, and Soul. This is the third year our church is hosting the retreat. It's always a fun time in the Lord."

Greg couldn't hold in his excitement. "And Glory will be speaking this year." He resembled a kid on Christmas morning. "Yep, on Saturday."

"Well, I can go." Ava paused, then addedd, "I need to go."

"I'm in." Toni interlocked her fingers with Eric's. "If he can make it without me for a weekend after the surprise I got for him."

Now, Eric was the kid looking under the Christmas tree. "What surprise? There's more?"

"Well, now hold on." Toni turned to Rene. "You in?"

Rene glanced at Paul, who nodded his head, smiling. She returned to the group and said, "Yes, I am."

Glory gave a small clap. "Yay! We can definitely get a discount on the rooms. My room is paid for, so we can have a mini road trip and make it a girls' weekend. It'll be fun. I'm excited."

Greg winked at her. "See, babe? Told you to just ask. I know you were worried about it being on such short notice, but you never know who may need to be there."

Rubbing his arm, Glory rested her head on her husband's shoulder. "You are so right. Thank you."

"Awesome." Eric slapped the table. "Now on to my surprise."

Toni grinned from ear to ear. "Okay. Well, Mr. Jacobs." She stood up at the table and took hold of his hand to stand beside her. "You're going to be a daddy!"

Eric's face lit up. "Are you for real?"

"Sure am. I thought I was pregnant, but the doctor confirmed it for me yesterday, just in time to surprise you for your birthday."

He picked her up as the guests clapped and cheered. "That is the best news ever, Toni. Thank you for making it so special for me. This is the best gift ever. I love you more and more every day."

"Eric, I love you too." Toni kissed him gently. "Now can you put me down, please?"

"Oh, oh, I'm so sorry. Are you okay? Maybe you should sit down." Eric was as nervous as any new father-to-be would be.

"Baby, I'm not carrying a glass egg. Well, maybe something that fragile, but I'm not going to break."

They both held each other with elated smiles across their faces.

Happy for the new parents-to-be, Ava raised her glass with the rest of the guests as Eric's brother led a toast for the couple. She wanted to be able to bring joy to Kevin like that. *Get him out of your head. He's not here and won't be in the days to come.*

With all the love being shared in the room, it was a positive place for Ava to be, but it only made her miss Kevin even more. Would they be able to get past this rough patch and move on? She needed the answer to that question to be a definite yes.

All of her hope was in Kevin, and in him being the last man she ever dated and eventually married. She wanted to know the answer to that question and several others. Like, how was Kevin doing? What was he doing? Was he thinking about Ava at all? And, probably the most important question of all, was he interested in returning to her anytime soon? He was more than likely distracted from all of the above and focused on finding his baby sister, but if he really loved Ava, he'd make room in his mind and in his heart for her. At least she hoped that would be the outcome.

Ava needed to stop focusing on herself. His sister was in real trouble. She could say a quick prayer for Tweet and think about someone else for a while. As she prayed right there at the dinner table, something came over her. An uneasy feeling set in. She should probably call Kevin to make sure everything was okay. Or would that just be another excuse to hear his voice? Another selfish act she should erase from her mind? *It couldn't hurt anyone to know how he's doing, right? What to do? What to do?*

Chapter Twenty

"Kevin? Is that you?"

"Yeah, Tweet, you called me." What was his baby sister on to where she didn't even know who she had dialed?

"Kevin, I need you to come get me."

The nervousness in her voice worried him. "Of course. Where are you?"

"Somewhere downtown. I don't know exactly where."

"Tweet, you gotta give me more than that." He tried to hide his frustration. "Who are you with? Do they know where you are? Tell me what's around you."

"I'm not really with anybody. I just need you to come get me. Please. Hurry."

"What happened to you staying in rehab this time, Tweet?"

"I had to leave there. I felt like I was going crazy. I just needed one more fix. But I promise to get off this stuff. I'll do whatever you and Momma want me to do. You can lock me in a room until I kick this habit for good. Just come get me this one last time. Please. I promise."

"I'm walking out the door right now." He snatched his keys off the kitchen counter. "I'll just head downtown and drive around until I see you. Just be there out in the open."

"Thank you, bro. Hey, I do know I passed that Chinese food place you took me to in order to get to this pay phone. I'll stay around here. Please just come get me. Hurry."

"Okay, I'm on my way, Tweet. Just stay where you are. Don't leave. I'll be there soon." He pushed the END button on his phone and hustled to his car. Getting to his sister was priority one. Could the Lord protect her from herself and others around her? Of course He could. But what would Tweet do that might get in the way of that? Would she even allow it to happen?

The drive to the downtown area gave Kevin a chance to reflect on some of the poor choices he had made in his younger . The biggest issue and what he wanted as a do-over more than anything else was to go back to the day he offered his baby sister her first drug. He'd come home from college for a visit, and he and his homeboy thought it was funny to let fifteen-year-old Tweet smoke marijuana with them. She hit the joint like a pro the first time and never looked back. He went back to college, and Tweet progressed to new experiences. He wasn't around to stop her. He left her on her own to decide what was wrong and right.

No one in the family ever blamed him for her drug abuse, at least not out loud anyway, but he knew if marijuana was the gateway drug, then he was the one who opened the gate for Tweet. He was the gatekeeper who ushered her down the destructive path, and that didn't sit well with him. He figured it didn't sit well with the rest of his family either. He blamed himself and no one else, not even Tweet.

He parked in front of the Chinese restaurant he'd taken her to for her last birthday. She loved Chinese food. That was one of many things they had in common. He got out of the car and then pushed his lock twice so the alarm would be heard by all the street folk who were posted up on the side streets. His car lights lit up the dark street with each beep.

The restaurant was clear of loiterers, but across the street, scruffy-looking people hung around in groups, smoking cigarettes. At least they looked like cigarettes. What was Tweet doing down there? Who could she be hanging out with down here? It wasn't a good place for her to be. She had a warm bed waiting for her at their mother's house and one at Kevin's house. He knew addicts couldn't see past their next hit, but he also knew she was so much better than those streets. The key was to get her to believe that. She couldn't see all of the people who wanted to help her.

Kevin walked to the end of the block, and when he didn't see a pay phone down the next cross street, he turned around and headed in the other direction. The crisp air forced him to lick his lips, but he wiped them when he remembered the possibility of getting chapped lips. He tried his best to look normal, but he knew real street folk could tell he had some fear in him. He never thought he would be back in a place like this again, but it was about Tweet, and he didn't care where he had to go to get her.

He wasn't sure what he would roll up on, and that was the scariest thought in his head at that moment. Tweet could be severely out of it, hurt, surrounded by other addicts or, worse, drug dealers. He needed to find her. He needed to protect her. Kevin felt a great need to save Tweet, since he was the one who started her off on her path of destruction.

After he passed his car for a second time, he yelled. "Tweet! Are you around here?"

With no answer, he continued on his trek down the congested street. The stench was real, as addicts received what they had been searching for from the guys on the street who supplied the demand. He took careful steps, keeping his eye on everyone he came close to. Trash blew across the street and blew over a homeless man. The man held a paper cup in the air and made eye contact with him. Kevin stuck his hand in his pocket and pulled out a few dollars he had forgotten about. He dropped the bills in the cup.

"God bless you, young brother. I appreciate the money, I do, but do you have anything that can get me high? Crack, heroin, I'll even take some weed. Anything, please."

"No, sir. I don't. But if you ever want to get off that stuff, you can call me." Kevin took a business card from the Christian Counseling Center out of his jacket pocket and dropped it in the cup as well. "Hope to see you there one day, brother."

"I hope so too." The man returned to leaning back into his spot.

Praying for the man as he continued searching for Tweet, Kevin felt hopeful. As he approached the alley, he heard some arguing down toward the end of it. Was that Tweet's voice? It had to be her voice. He knew her voice. Kevin was wary about where the sounds were coming from.

A gunshot rang out from down the alley. Kevin shuffled toward the alley as two thugged-out dudes ran past him, abruptly brushing his shoulder. "Hey! Hold on."

They hit the corner and disappeared into the night. He turned back to see the victim sprawled out on the ground. As he ran toward the figure, he kept repeating, "Please don't be Tweet. Please don't be Tweet. Please, God."

His baby sister lay there holding her stomach.

He knelt down beside her. "Tweet, it's Kevin, your big brother. Do you hear me? I'm here, Tweet. I'm here."

She did her best to lift her head. "Kev? Is that you?"

"Yeah, I'm here." Kevin sat down deeper into the muggy ground as he tried to keep her head resting on his knee.

"He shot me, Kev. He shot me. I wasn't gonna keep it all. I was just gonna use a little bit. Just a little and that was gonna be it, Kev. I swear."

He pulled out his cell phone and dialed 911. After giving the dispatcher their location, he returned his focus to Tweet. "Stay up. Talk to me, Tweet." His hand, covered in blood, rested on top of hers to help put pressure on the wound. It didn't seem to be working. There was blood everywhere. It seemed like it was a running faucet that wouldn't shut off.

Tweet closed her eyes.

"Tweet. I need you to stay up until the ambulance gets here." Tears started to form in his eyes. He begged God silently to keep her with him.

"I'm up. I'm up."

"Good. Now talk to me." He struggled to be stern.

She struggled but spoke through coughs. "I do have something to tell you."

"What is it, baby girl? Talk to me."

Tweet rubbed his face while her eyes glazed over. "I know you blame yourself for my addiction."

"I do. I can't help it." He shook his head in agreement as he applied more pressure to where the blood flowed from. "What type of brother am I to give you your first hit of any drug?"

"You gotta know it's not your fault, Kev. I would've found my way to drugs one way or the other. I'm an addict and that's it. Don't blame yourself." She dropped her head.

"Tweet. Stay with me. Tweet." Kevin heard sirens in the distance as others on the street started to hover around them. A concerned bystander threw him a towel. He nodded and pressed the towel over her bullet wound.

"I'm here, bro." She coughed and gasped for air. "Tell Momma I'm sorry."

"Don't talk like that, Tweet." He sniffled. "You can tell her yourself."

"I don't think so." She stared into his eyes. "And, Kevin, I'm sorry I couldn't get clean. I know you did everything you knew to do. It just wasn't in me." Blood spurted out as she tried to control her cough. "I love you, bro. Always have and always will. It didn't matter to me how you were."

Tears fell from his eyes. "I love you too, Tweet. Please just hold on a little bit longer. The ambulance is almost here. Please, Tweet. I'm not ready to let you go. Please, Tweet. Please."

Her body went limp. She felt heavier in his arms. Kevin cried out as he hugged her tight. He gently placed her on the ground and closed her eyes. The paramedics ran to him and knelt down beside them.

Kevin stood. "It's too late. She's gone."

"Sir, please, we can still try." One of the paramedics started to cut through her shirt and pulled out stickers to apply to Tweet's chest, while the other hooked up the wires to a defibrillator. They both cleared the body, and one of them pushed the lighted button. The first shock went through, causing her to jerk off the ground. The paramedics waited for a few seconds, watching the screen.

At that point, Kevin was hopeful. Maybe, just maybe, it would work and this would be the sure wakeup call she needed. Kevin silently prayed. He stood to the side, watching their efforts to bring his sister back to life. After three shocks, they looked to him, shaking their heads.

"I'm sorry, sir. We did all we could."

Kevin wanted to scream, shake his sister out of the death within her. If only he'd been just a few minutes earlier, he could have stopped it all. There was nothing he could do to bring her back. He took a few steps away from her body and then took out his cell. Kevin took a deep breath. He was about to make the phone call to his mother he had always feared he'd have to make one day.

The phone rang five times before she picked up. "Hello."

"Momma, is anyone there with you?"

"Kevin? No, why? What's wrong?"

Kevin did the best he could to hold back his tears with a calm voice. "Nothing, Momma. I'll be there in a few."

"Okay, son, I'll see you soon."

He hung up the phone. Kevin couldn't tell her over the phone, especially since no one was with her. He quickly dialed his sister Martha.

She picked up on the first ring. "Hey, bro, what's up?"

"Martha, Tweet is no longer with us. She has gone home." He waited before saying anything else.

"Kevin, what do you mean? What happened?"

"Martha, Tweet is gone. She's dead. Please get over to Momma's. I haven't told her yet. Get Mary and get over to Momma's. I'll be there shortly. I just have to see where Tweet's body will be."

Martha's words were hard to understand through her sobs. "Kevin . . . Kevin . . . no . . . no! You're wrong. Please tell me you're wrong. . . . Please."

Fighting his own tears back, he pleaded, "Martha, please get Mary and go to Momma's house. I'll be there shortly. Now just do what I say. Go to Momma's house now." Kevin hung up the phone before he lost it.

Officers were now on the scene, asking questions to the bystanders huddling around his dead sister. He approached one of the officers. "Excuse me. Can you tell me where she will be going?"

"And you are?"

"I'm her brother."

"Did you see what happened?" The officer pulled out a pad to write on.

"I was too late. When I arrived, a group of men rushed past me after I heard the gunshot. When I got to her, she was bleeding. Then I dialed 911. The paramedics arrived and they tried to revive her, but it was too late."

"Do you know why she was here? This place is known for local drug addicts and dealers. Was she into drugs?"

"Yes, she was an addict. I don't know what she was doing here. She called me to come get her, and that's why I was here." Kevin looked over and saw his sister being zipped up into a black body bag. "Can you please tell me where they're taking her?"

"They will be taking her to the coroner's office for an autopsy, since there will be an investigation. Her body will be released to the family once that happens."

Kevin gave the officer his information and left the scene. When he got into his car, tears started to wet his face. "God, why her? Why now? I was going to save her." He banged his fist against the steering wheel. "Why? Why?"

He leaned over the steering wheel and began to speak to the Lord. "God, I don't understand. Was I not doing everything I could? I did everything I could. Why did it have to end this way?" As he continued to ask questions, a warm feeling came over him. He looked up and saw the clear skies above. It was as if God was speaking to him. He closed his eyes and took in the warm feeling. There was a weight lifted from him. He was no longer crying but smiling.

"Thank you. How could I have doubted you? You are the only one who knew what was best for Tweet. She is in your hands now. I know she will forever be safe and free of all that holds her down. I understand now. She is free, finally. Thank you, Heavenly Father. Thank you."

He wiped his face and started his car. On the way to his mother's, nothing but good memories came to mind about Tweet. By the time he pulled into his mother's driveway, his spirit was ready to break the news to his mother. Kevin parked behind his sisters and turned off the ignition. As he approached the house, he could hear the screams of pain from his mother and sisters.

He took a deep breath and whispered, "God, I know you will be with me, and we will all get through this together."

Chapter Twenty-one

The women's retreat couldn't have come at a better time. Ava looked forward to spending the weekend with her three closest friends in the world and, hopefully, putting tormenting thoughts of how she messed things up with Kevin on hold. Or, even let go of them for good. It was something she really didn't want to do, but she knew it was the only way to start moving forward.

That would be a hard task to accomplish with Rene and Toni both being dropped off at Glory's house by their significant others, and Glory's family in the driveway seeing her off, while Ava parked her car on the street. Instead of focusing on the negative, though, she promised herself she'd have a positive outlook on this weekend, so things could possibly change. She'd just enjoy the people who were there and wouldn't worry about those who weren't.

When Glory's twins, Hannah and Micah, saw Ava get out of the car and open her trunk, they ran down the driveway. "Ava!" They supplied her with much-needed hugs. Their tiny little arms squeezed her tight. She hadn't seen them since Christmas, and it seemed they missed her. At least somebody did.

As the four ladies loaded up in Glory's Mercedes-Benz SUV, Ava knew God's hand had orchestrated this getaway for this time in her life. She needed to be around other women who may have gone through what she was experiencing, and they would be able to offer her advice. She'd get the chance to lean on them for comfort.

Ava needed to get out of her environment for a few days, let go of her negative thoughts, take some things to the Lord, and return refreshed. That was her hope anyway. That was her hope for all of her girlfriends, because even though everything on the surface looked peachy for the moment, she knew Rene, Toni, and Glory all had their individual inner struggles, just as she did. They all needed to receive whatever God had in store for them and their situations. They would hopefully get the chance to really "breathe."

During the entire trip to the hotel, they shared details of their lives, hopes, and dreams. They discussed how God had been moving in their circumstances, but how they all needed more answers. It was great to be able to share and relate to one another. Ava cherished that time with her girls and would be sure to include that time in her journal writing that night.

Glory turned to Ava and smiled. "Y'all will absolutely love Pastor Clara. She brings the Word in a real practical way for you, snd she has always been transparent with her own life. She's helped me a great deal."

"Looking forward to it." Ava wasn't lying. She needed this to be a miracle retreat and give her the tools to mend her relationship with the love of her life.

"So what else can we expect besides a great Word?" Toni asked from the back seat.

"Let's see . . . This is only my second time attending, but the goal is definitely to feed your mind, body, and soul. You can expect awesome worship, some sort of craft thing, prayer time, both group and individual, and we exercise and take walks together." Glory's excitement spilled out into the car. "Oh, and last year, they had a chair masseuse available if you wanted it. And the food. Don't even get me started on that. Too good."

Rene said, "Just great. It all sounds wonderful. I hope with all that you just mentioned, I also get some wisdom for my relationship with Paul."

Glory offered a retreat tip: "Whatever you do, just be open to how God will move this weekend, and you never know what can happen. I've seen it happen before, and He is no respecter of persons, so it can happen for all of us."

"Won't He do it?" Toni yelled.

The group shared a laugh. Ava knew she was headed to the right place at the right time. She was definitely open to God's plan. Would He speak to her, or was she too much of a hot, emotional mess to be able to hear from Him clearly? All she could do at this point was show up. So that was her plan, and she was sticking to it.

After they had all checked in and gotten settled into their rooms, they headed to the auditorium for dinner. The place was adorned with a pink-and-gold décor, welcoming to a woman's eye, as the inviting smell from the kitchen reminded Ava of being at home, preparing a feast for her family and friends.

Glory was right about the food. The stuffed chicken breast was glorious. With every bite of the melted cheese and seasoned veggies that hid inside the succulent piece of meat, Ava was overjoyed that her appetite had returned.

As dinner came to a close, Pastor Clara scampered to the stage to welcome all the ladies and invite everyone to the front for worship. When the first beat dropped in the up-tempo praise song, Ava was consumed by the presence of God. He'd brought her there for a reason.

She prayed that her heart would be open to whatever work He wanted to perform in her over the course of the next couple of days. Needing Him in every area of her life, she silently welcomed Him into any area He wanted to enter. He could turn things around. She wanted more than anything to believe that. By the time the last song was belted out, Lauren Daigle's "How Can It Be," Ava was on her knees, wiping the tears that ran down her cheeks. It was moving to her.

Pastor Clara spoke a prayer of blessing over all the attendees, asking God to show the ladies what they needed to let go of in their pasts to be able to move forward in all parts of their lives.

After allowing all the ladies to take their seats, Pastor Clara grabbed her Bible and stood in front of the podium. "Please turn to Matthew 6:33–34." She flipped through her pages until she arrived at her destination. "I'm sure you have read this scriptur, or at least heard it before, but have you ever really studied the words and taken them all in? *Seek first the Kingdom of God and His righteousness, and all these things shall be added unto you.*"

Ava knew that scripture very well. Had she always believed the words, or was she guilty of making the words work for how she'd wanted her situation to turn out? That was another whole story. More than anything, she wanted God's story for her life.

"God's Word is saying not to worry about your current circumstances or what you've gone through in the past. Keep your eyes on Him, and He will take care of your future."

A "Hallelujah" was shouted from the back, along with a few "Amen."

"This evening, I'm going to have you do an exercise." The audience gasped. Pastor grinned. "Not physical exercise. I heard some of you lose your breath when I said exercise. But no, that's tomorrow. And we won't let Angela hurt you too bad."

The resident Zumba instructor stood up and waved as some ladies cheered and chuckles flowed through the crowd as well.

"No, tonight I want all of us to take some paper and write down what you need to let go of. The ladies will come around and give paper to those who need it." She waved her hand for the ushers to fill the aisles.

"What thoughts, be it about your past, present, or future, have been a source of concern or worry for you? What do you need to give to God once and for all? That destructive relationship, a sickness, an addiction, any type of abuse? He can handle anything you give to Him. He is a God who can turn your situation around with the snap of His fingers. Won't you let Him do it? Give all your worries, concerns, temptations to Him. He will handle it."

Women who needed paper held their hands up high, seemingly reaching for the peace this activity could bring. Glory, Rene, and Toni were focused on whatever words they were scribbling on their paper. Ava listed her main concerns. She was almost certain there were more, but her and Kevin's relationship and her relationship with his family claimed the top of the list. After a pause, she also added the fact that all she focused on lately was being married, and she hated on those who were getting married. Ava didn't want to, but she rarely thought of anything else.

The room was mostly quiet as only soft music played in the background while the women wrote, so when the booming sound came of the ushers opening the large French doors to the patio of the auditorium, the noise startled Ava. She was a bit hesitant, because she did not know what she was expected to do. Would she have to recite her list to these strangers? She didn't want all her business out there like that. It was between her and God. No one else. A steel trashcan sat in the middle of the concrete slab just outside the doors.

"In Bible days, some believed that fire could symbolize a sort of cleansing or purification. We're going to roll with that idea and use the fire as a visual to allow your concerns to be removed forever." Pastor Clara nodded in the direction of the usher standing next to the trashcan. "Go ahead, Marilyn."

Just then, Marilyn took out a lighter and put flame to a piece of paper; then she tossed it into the can. She added some lighter fluid. The sudden blaze caused her and another usher to step back as the flame brightened up the inside of the dim auditorium.

"All right, the ushers will escort you all row by row to walk by the fire. When you arrive to the flame, toss your paper in the trashcan and say good-bye to your worries and concerns."

A few women yelled out words of praise.

"And on your way back in the building, please pick up a small gift. I have a journal for each one of you. I want you to write positive thoughts on what you desire for God to do in your life, and praises for all He has already done and will do in your life. You'll drop off your problems or issues in the fire and pick up a journal, symbolizing you picking up the peace that surpasses all understanding."

"Amen." Ava couldn't contain her feelings anymore. She was relieved that throwing her paper into the fire would lift the weight that consumed her. At least she believed it would be a start. She had an open mind, for it was God who wanted her there for a reason.

"After you receive your journal, you may return to your rooms, or feel free to stay here. I just suggest that you get with God and pray, worship, write in your journal, whatever, but don't miss out on this opportunity to go deeper with the Lord. I know God will do great things, and there'll be many testimonies to come from this simple act of faith." Pastor lifted her hand in praise.

"And remember, the God you serve is a miracle-working Father, and He wants to give you all the desires of your heart. In His timing. Trust that He is a good God and has not forgotten about you."

Glory passed the box of Kleenex down their row. Ava took a few and wiped her tears. She did believe that God had forgotten about her in certain areas of her life. She would give that and much more to Him and walk away with His peace.

As the women started filing into the aisle and walking in line toward the patio, the worship pastor began playing a song Ava recognized at the first note. The same powerful soloist who had opened the service took hold of the microphone and put her beautiful voice to Tamela Mann's "Take Me to the King." That song and its commanding lyrics had helped Ava through many tough times. The scene was overwhelming.

Each of the ladies split up and explored their relationship with the Lord in different ways. Ava, emotionally drained, wrote everything she felt and whatever popped into her mind in her journal. After about thirty minutes of writing and praying, she fell asleep. Finally her thoughts were at peace.

The next morning, the group of ladies woke up refreshed and joined the nature walk before breakfast. As the ladies walked and talked, Ava was sure to take in all the breathtaking scenery. As the sun peeked through the tall, mature trees, it shone on the beautiful simplicity of the morning. Birds chirping, morning dew dripping from the leaves, and the fresh morning were all added to the calm scene that Ava couldn't get enough of.

She was proud that she could walk the two-and-a-half mile hike without her back hurting. She would continue to walk and work out when she could. Dance classes were her favorite. Ava would be moving and burning calories, yet having fun. She cherished the exercise she did get in, which proved to be more than beneficial. She'd stick with what worked. Not recognizing her own change in attitude toward working out, she was grateful it did take place.

The late morning hours included a craft class. Ava's painted pottery plate didn't look all that great, but the friendly women complimented her anyway. She painted the white plate with bold purple and green colors. She already had a place to put it in her apartment. Well, only if it passed the final test when she placed it on the shelf. If it stood out like a sore thumb, then the piece would have to stay in the box she was to carry it in.

The time spent with the other ladies was therapeutic. Thoughts of Kevin dropped in and out of her head, but she disciplined herself to concentrate on what was in front of her. And right then, it wasn't Kevin. She wanted to talk to him and see him but knew this time away could work in her favor. It was time for both of them to really miss one another. When they did return to one another, hopefully, they'd appreciate each other's company that much more.

By lunchtime, Ava was starving and looked forward to the grub placed in front of her. One of her favorites, smoked salmon, sat on a bed of grilled vegetables and a hefty salad with Italian dressing.

A Zumba class was next on the schedule for those who weren't interested in trying the ropes course. Ava was in the best shape of her life, but she wasn't about to dangle twenty to thirty feet in the air. Pleased that she could complete the one-hour class minus the back and knee pain, she couldn't help but reflect on how far she had come physically. God had been working on the inside and outside of her, and she felt the results. Her confidence was at an all-time high.

The nutrition class followed the exercise session. Ava could barely keep up with all the ideas that ran through her head about her dream of owning a restaurant. Her Manna Catering gig was doing fairly well, and she kept saying every year was the year she'd draw up the business plan and make a real go for the restaurant. Once she heard of all the ways to make simple, small changes to make healthier foods taste better, she dang near caught a hand cramp from writing her thoughts down so fast. Ava didn't want to forget anything. God had placed that dream in her heart for a reason, and she was going to do her part to have it come to pass.

She would go ahead and send in the papers on Monday. Ava had gotten as close as filing all the paperwork with the bank for a business loan, yet she never followed through. She felt she'd get turned down, but all she could do was try. If it turned out to be a no, then Ava would have to accept it and try again, until God willed His power for her to get a yes.

Saturday afternoon offered the ladies some free time. Glory napped before she was to speak that night, while Ava, Rene, and Toni headed to the auditorium for fifteen-minute chair massages. If there had been any stress left after the previous night, it was gone once Ava stood up from the chair.

That evening, Ava knew it must've helped Glory a great deal to release some junk the night before. She'd heard Glory speak before as her patient in her group sessions, but Glory was on fire that night. Her message focus was about how to walk by faith and not by sight. Ava recorded 2 Corinthians 5:7 in her journal.

More tears were shed as an emotional weight was lifted off Ava with one of Glory's most meaningful statements. When Glory spoke the words, "It may be your time but not your turn," Ava came unglued. That was exactly what she needed to hear. Her time was now, and she believed that with all of her heart; but it wasn't her turn to get married. It was her cousin's turn, coworker's turn, and now Rene's turn. She needed to be happy for them and trust in the Father who knew best. Ava needed to wait until God said it was her turn, and she could live with that.

That Sunday morning, after a time of prayer and worship, the ladies headed back to Houston. Small talk was made on the way to the retreat, but on the way home, God's glory in what He had done in them over the course of the weekend shone bright.

Toni interlocked her fingers and rested them in her lap. "Basically, I realized I can't put my trust in Eric. I must continue to put it in the Lord. I've said that before, I know, but it's simple. Either I am going to do what I need to do to make this work, or I'm not. He's serving God now, and I know the Lord has a hold on him. Not to mention, Eric is over the moon about becoming a father. Friday, I let our past go, so from here on out, I move forward, trusting God will protect my family from any plans of the enemy."

"Amen, Toni." Rene patted her on the leg. "Well, for me, I also let go of the past on Friday. I cannot hesitate on something good with Paul because I'm fearful of diving all in because of how Ishmael treated me."

Ava cringed at hearing Ishmael's name.

Rene went on. "Just because he continues to send me letters doesn't mean I have to open them. That chapter of my life is closed, and I need to finally close the door once and for all."

"Hallelu-yur, Rene." Toni giggled.

"In fact, I was thinking of going to visit him in jail."

Toni looked confused. "Wait, what? How did you come to that conclusion after this weekend?"

Rene laughed. "No, it's not what you think. To go and just be straight up with him. To face my past and put it to rest finally." Rene leaned forward to touch Ava's shoulder. "Ava, would you go with me?"

A silence filled the car as if everyone was imagining the dynamic of that trio together again.

As weird as the request was, Rene could ask anything of Ava in that circumstance and she would do it to continue to foster amends between them and that situation. "Of course, but I really don't know why."

"I want you there to face your past too. I think if we both face him together, it would make the big elephant in the room disappear."

"Rene, I thought you forgave me and let that go when you put him in jail."

"I'm not saying I didn't. All I'm saying is this will free me of my insecurities of you."

Ava was confused and couldn't understand what Rene was trying to say. "What do you mean by that?"

"I've never told you this, but after everything that happened, I felt funny speaking to you about Paul."

"Do you still think what happened between me and Ishmael was on purpose? Is that why you wanted to keep your engagement from me?" Ava was trying her best to keep her voice at a calm tone.

"No. Not anymore. I know it wasn't on purpose. It was your lonely, broken heart causing you all the pain, and Ishmael took advantage of that. I know and understand that now. As for my engagement, that was all me. My insecurities of the unknown. Not knowing if I was making the right decision."

Ava didn't know if she should be mad or happy about Rene's revealing truths about her.

"Are you mad at me, Ava? I don't want you to be upset. I just wanted it off my chest. This entire weekend helped me to believe that with God's help I could let this out, and you as my friend will understand why." Rene's eyes began to tear up.

Ava hugged Rene tightly. "Of course I understand; and as God had brought you back into my life, I believe it was His will to bring us closer. I love you, Rene."

There was not a dry eye in the car. Everyone realized their friendships were a beautiful, uplifting relationship throughout all the trials of difficult events.

After all tears were wiped away, Rene bellowed, "I love you girls too. You guys will forever be in my life, whether it may be bad or the best. I'm truly thankful and happy God put all of you in my life."

"Okay, I think I can speak for all of us that this weekend was an awakening for each one of us. And our bond with each other grew even tighter. Now I don't want to cry anymore. I want to laugh and smile with my girls."

"As do I," Toni spoke.

"So now it's my turn." Glory bubbled with excitement. "Well, for me, I know I need to do my best to truly respect Greg. I have my moments when I can be a real wench to him, and I know that's not right. He is trying his best, and it doesn't help him one bit for me to be so negative and careless with my words, so I let go of that."

"Awesome. It's wonderful to hear that." It was now Ava's opportunity to share. "Well, Glory, speaking of your words, I loved that phrase you used about 'it may be your time, but not your turn.' That could go for Greg as well. The right job is coming soon. I just know it."

"Amen." Glory winked at Ava.

"And for me, one thing is I got some great ideas for my restaurant-to-be. I'm going to stop procrastinating and apply for that loan, and whatever it brings, it brings. I will leave it in God's hands."

The three ladies cheered.

Toni said, "You go, Ms. Ava. That's what I'm talking about."

"Thank you." Ava smiled. "And then, secondly, I realized that I've been so focused on getting married, I can barely enjoy the relationship I'm in. Or was in. I know God has a plan. I just need to rest in that and quit trying to force things on my own. I love Kevin and do not want to push him away, so I burned that issue away in the flame and picked up God's peace on the way out."

It seemed all of the ladies had a productive weekend emotionally and spiritually. Ava believed that change had taken place and she was grateful. She had moved forward individually. Her only question now was how could she move forward with Kevin? If she still had a chance, she would leave that timing in God's hands too.

Chapter Twenty-two

Sitting across the thick glass from Ishmael, Ava could think of a million and one other places she'd rather be at that moment. But right then, Rene needed her, so the only place she needed to be was by her side. Rene's emotions were hard to read. Ava would be there for whatever. Whether tears were shed, curse words shared, or a harsh attitude shown, Ava would support her best friend however she could.

Rene stared at him, sitting like a statue. Ishmael's elation poured out of his smile. He picked up the phone first, seemingly excited to get the visit he had probably been wanting for a while. Rene slowly took the phone off the hook as if she wasn't sure she was doing the right thing. She looked to Ava briefly. With Ava's smile and nod she knew she was doing the right thing. This was a door that had to be closed.

"I've been good." Rene's tone was solemn. "Actually, great." She tried to pep it up a bit. "So how have you been, Ishmael?"

Being able to hear only her friend's words, Ava, who sat facing away from the distraught pair, focused on others in the room.

Rene cleared her throat and took a deep breath. "I need you to quit sending me letters, Ishmael. We are done. This chapter is over, and I am not turning back the pages on anything between us."

Although she didn't care to make eye contact with him, Ava turned to read Ishmael's body language. He threw his hands up. Rene shook her head to whatever his request was.

Rene spoke with assurance. "I'm moving on, and I need you to do the same. I do not want to be a part of your life or you a part of mine."

Whatever words he said, his serious facial expression added to the drama of the moment. Ava had never seen that look on his face as long as she had known him.

"I'm sorry, Ishmael. I don't love you anymore. There is nothing you can do to bring that love back."

His puppy dog eyes pleaded his case through the glass.

Rene, sighing, shrugged her shoulders and turned to Ava. "He asked me to put you on the phone."

Not sure what he was up to, Ava paused and then took the bait. As Rene handed her the phone, Ava's emotional guard rose. "Yes?"

He spoke from behind what was still a handsome face; it just had a hardness added to it now. Looking straight into her eyes, he said, "Ava, I just wanted to say I'm truly sorry for putting you in harm's way. I realize now I was upset with myself and did everything in my power to blame other people. I thought it was the right thing to do. I was being selfish and stupid."

Ava shook her head. "I played my part too." She said that more for Rene's benefit than Ishmael's.

"Yeah, but I took things way too far with the accident and all the damage it caused you afterward. I hope you can find it in your heart to forgive me."

She looked at Rene. "I appreciate your apology, and I have already forgiven you."

"You have?" His eyebrows rose.

"Yes, mainly because that frees me, but I can't forget, and neither will Rene. So if you care about her at all, you will leave her alone. If you love her like you say, then let her go. She's happier without you."

He said nothing but nodded for Ava to give the phone back to Rene. This would be the last time she ever followed a direction of his. She wanted to get an attitude, as she loathed him for what he represented in her life; but she had made it through it all, thanks to God, and she wasn't going to hang in the past. It wasn't good for her or Rene. Ava handed the phone back to her friend and turned away from Ishmael.

Rene put her hand over the phone and held it away from her body and leaned closer to Ava, as if he could hear through the glass. "I think I should tell him about Paul and maybe he'll get the picture. What do you think?"

"I think you should do whatever you think you need to do." Ava looked at Ishmael. "He can take it. And if he can't, he'll just have to deal with it. That's not your concern anymore."

Placing the phone over her ear, Rene locked eyes with Ishmael. "I have something to tell you, and I just need you to listen."

He nodded his head.

"I have been dating a friend of mine I have known for. I love him, and he recently proposed." She paused as if to let those words sink in. "And I said yes. The wedding is this Saturday. In Jamaica."

Ishmael's face fell. His words changed Rene's sitting position, and she looked uneasy.

"Yes, I'm very happy. I just wanted you to know and hear it from me. This will be our last contact. If you send any more letters, I won't read them out of respect for him. I wish you the best. Take care." Rene placed the phone back on the hook and stood up.

Ishmael watched Rene walk away through tearful eyes.

Ava turned to catch up with her girlfriend. "Do you think he'll adhere to your wishes?"

"Not sure, but I'm serious. I can't let him hold me back from what Paul and I can have, so I hope he does and is able to move on himself. That'll be best for both of us. If he doesn't, there's always a restraining order that will make him adhere." She chuckled at the thought.

Best for both of us. What was best for all of them? Rene and Ava's relationship had been restored, and with Ishmael totally out of the picture, not reminding Rene of the past, things would only get better for all of them involved.

"Wanna get a bite to eat?" Rene seemed upbeat and finally free of her past.

"Yeah, I'm down. Where you wanna go?"

"Doesn't matter, girl."

"Okay, we can drive until something speaks to us." Spending more time with Rene would be just what Ava needed. Her mind had a break from thoughts of Kevin. She wanted to talk to him more than anything, but didn't want to break down and call him again. Hanging with Rene would keep her busy and off her phone.

She hadn't spoken to him in a while, and with getting ready to head to Jamaica for Rene and Paul's nuptials, Ava would've loved to invite Kevin along, but if he refused the invitation, Ava didn't know if her heart could take it. She wasn't courageous enough to find out.

Rene drove toward downtown Houston. An Italian bistro, Little Italy, right outside of the city spoke to them. They situated themselves on the patio to soak up the Texas sun. Ava wouldn't bring up their visit with Ishmael. If Rene wanted to talk about it, she was game to, but there was no need to open the door to the awkward subject herself. The door was completely closed in Ava's mind.

Rene stood up quickly. "I don't even know why I sat down. I knew I had to go to the restroom."

Ava giggled. "Go 'head, girl. Do what you gotta do. Want me to order for you if the waitress comes by?"

"Yes, thank you." Rene straightened out her skirt. "I'll just have the grilled chicken salad. You know how I eat it."

"Yeah, I do. I gotcha."

Rene always leaned to the healthier side of life, and Ava joined her sometimes, but not that day. She was sitting in a place with some of the finest authentic pasta in town, and she'd be sure to get her portion of it while she was there.

As she waited to see who showed up first, the waitress or Rene, she took out her cell phone, hoping she had missed a call or text she didn't hear when she walked into the restaurant. But there was nothing. She tapped on her Yahoo! e-mail app and waited for it to pull up across the screen. Scrolling down to find something that looked important, she was interrupted by the waitress.

"Hello, ma'am." A young woman spoke through tight, bouncy blond curls. She couldn't be more than nineteen or twenty, and calling Ava "ma'am" like she was an old lady. "Are y'all ready to order now?"

"Yes. My friend will have the grilled chicken salad with light ranch and extra olives." She skimmed the pasta choices one last time. "And I'll have the shrimp and chicken carbonara."

"One of my favorites." The waitress smiled as she wrote down the order.

"And I'd like to add mushrooms to it please." Ava could taste the first bite already as she anticipated the arrival of her meal. She always ordered the same thing at every restaurant, and that last bite of whatever the special of the day was returned to her mind when she walked back through the doors of the restaurant.

Ava returned her focus to her e-mail. In her inbox, a couple of e-mails from Bank of Texas were in the list. A nervous excitement rose in her. This could be the business loan approval information she'd been waiting for.

As she read the first line, her heart fell. The first word that stood out to her was "unfortunately." She looked at the bottom. It was signed by Johnny Richards, her loan officer. She didn't need to read any further. Maybe she needed to close the door on her restaurant dream like Rene had closed the door on Ishmael. Nothing seemed to work out for her in that respect, so maybe she needed to get a new dream; but she loved to cook for and serve others. She had to keep trying.

It would've been nice to be able to lean on Kevin's shoulder in that moment. Ava was sure that he would've offered the perfect words of encouragement to lift her up. He was special like that. She missed him. She needed him. Most of all, she loved him, and with the absence of communication at that time in their relationship, Ava hoped he didn't forget that. Or forget her altogether.

Chapter Twenty-three

The scene in Jamaica was like something right out of a movie: clear ocean waters, the sweet smell of mangoes, and the beautiful array of colors displayed around the resort. Could Ava get her groove back? Even though she was surrounded by the beautiful, scenic views, a certain sadness loomed over her. At least as she stood at the altar in the two previous weddings when she was a bridesmaid, Ava could find peace in Kevin's eyes as he gazed into hers.

With him not in her life now, she could only be partly excited for her friend, but since this trip was for Rene, she'd do her best to focus on that part of the weekend and be there for her friend during what promised to be one of the most special occasions in her life. She hadn't talked to Kevin in a while. The silence between them was killing her, so sitting on the patio of their resort and drinking anything with alcohol in it as she watched the waves crashing against the white beaches was the best remedy she could come up with.

Toni and Eric lounged in the chairs beside her. Rene needed some alone time and a nap. Her emotions were running high. Cold feet, maybe, but it was more like uncontrolled excitement mixed with mild anxiety. Paul had taken care of everything, so all she had to do was try on dresses out of the half dozen he'd sent to her room, choose one, and chill the rest of the night. After the dress was chosen, she told Ava and Toni she just needed some time alone to pray.

Ava, the third wheel, needed to find something to do. "Hey, you two."

Toni lifted her shades and sat up. "What's up, girl?"

"I think I'm gonna go get a massage." Ava batted her eyes and tilted her head.

"Ooh, that sounds nice."

Eric put his drink down. "You want us to go with you?"

Then I'd still be the third wheel. "No, it's quite all right. You two enjoy this amazing, romantic setting."

Toni gave a shot at comforting her friend. "Ava, I'm sorry you're upset about Kevin, but you should hang out with us and not by yourself. We're family and want to be here for you."

"I know, girl, and I do appreciate that, but I think a massage will do me some good." Ava finished off the rest of her drink. "It'll help me relax."

"I getcha, girl. Eric and I will be here if you need us."

"Okay, but I'll probably just go up to my room after the massage and catch y'all in the morning." *Or see how many drinks it takes to get the courage to call Kevin.*

Ava hugged Toni and Eric and sauntered away. She stopped at the bar on the way to the front desk of the massage parlor. Waiting her turn, she knew this was exactly what she needed. Soft music would be playing as her tensed muscles were rubbed by a nice-looking Jamaican man. He didn't even have to be nice looking. A man would do, period. She missed Kevin's touch, and this relaxing massage would kill two birds with one stone.

"Ma'am, may I help you?" The desk attendant smiled under dark, bushy eyebrows.

Ava woke up out of her fantasy, ready for the real thing. "Uh, yes. I wanted to see if you had any open appointments for this evening for a massage."

"Let me see here." The clerk pulled one of her thick black locks out of her face to look over the rim of her pink-tinted glasses. "Looks like you're in luck. We were totally booked, but we had a last-minute cancellation. Ooh, and it's with one of our best massage therapists, Dexter. He's great with Swedish relaxation massages."

"Sounds perfect." The fact that he was a he was what sounded perfect. Ava looked forward to getting comfortable on that table.

"Okay, great. The time slot is at nine o'clock. His last appointment for the night. That's about an hour away, so you can wait in our waiting room, or feel free to go out to the bar. You just need to come back about ten minutes beforehand and fill out some paperwork."

Ava knew herself very well. "Can I fill it out now? After a few more drinks, I may not be able to give you my best handwriting."

The clerk giggled. "I understand."

As she filled out the medical release form and massage preferences sheet, she contemplated whether she should really go through with it. She'd already had three drinks on the patio, and another hour of drinking in front of her before a man was to put his hands on her body might not be the healthiest move for her and Kevin's relationship. *Wait a minute. What relationship?* He had left her to fend for herself.

Ava handed the clerk the clipboard with completed forms, promised her she'd be back in time, and then headed back to the bar. She found an open barstool and ordered a John Daly. Sure, a tropical drink in a tropical place would be typical, but she was feeling anything but typical at that moment. She needed vodka.

As she sipped the sweet, cool drink, she couldn't help but think of Kevin. How was he? How was his family? Shoot, where was he? She missed him something awful, but he obviously didn't feel the same about her. Why hadn't he called? Didn't he even care how she was doing?

Maybe he never did, and that's why it was so easy for him to rid his mind of her. Did he ever really love her?

Ava absolutely stunk it up in the relationship area of her life. If she wasn't trying to hold on to the bad men she'd been in a relationship with, she was pushing away the good ones. Maybe she was destined to be alone forever. That would definitely be easier, but also very lonely. She could work out her relationship issues during her hour-long massage. Better yet, she could put all of her stresses aside and just enjoy the experience for what it was. The latter sounded better.

By the time Ava's hour of drinking at the bar was up, she and John Daly had reacquainted themselves several times over. She glided to the peaceful waiting area until Dexter arrived. Melting back into the plush couch, she closed her eyes and took in the sounds around her. The speaker above her head shared soft, calming string instruments, while the water fountain flirted with her mind. She could take a nap right there, but she didn't want to miss the main attraction of the massage therapist's touch.

"Ava?"

She opened her eyes to find a six foot two chocolate muscular frame standing in front of her. He wore long dreads that were pulled back in a thick ponytail, which allowed his bright smile to be showcased.

"Yes." She stood and walked toward the male model.

"How are you this evening?" His strong Jamaican accent added to his appeal.

"Good. A bit stressed earlier, but I can't remember what about now." She laughed.

"Well, good. Hopefully, I can help you wipe whatever it was from your mind completely."

You sure can try. Ava followed Dexter back to his room. The back view was just as put together as the front view. After she entered the room, she put her purse down and began taking off her sandals. The massage table was draped with brown blankets that helped to darken the room and complemented the mocha-colored walls. A small water fountain was displayed that shone a small light from behind it. Over her head, the soft tempo of the music trickled down into her soul. She felt more relaxed by just walking into the room. The massage may throw her over the top.

"Okay, I guess you know the drill." He grinned.

"Yep, I do. Plus, I'm a little hot. Just came from the bar. The drinks are catching up with me." She giggled like a schoolgirl.

"Well, take your time. I'm in no rush. You're my last massage for the night." Dexter looked at her paperwork. "Are there any special areas you want me to focus on?"

"Nope, not really. Just need to relax."

"I can definitely help you with that." He dimmed the lights. "I'll leave you for a few minutes so you can go ahead and dress down to what you feel comfortable in; and when I return, I'll get started."

"Okay, thank you."

As Ava took off every piece of clothing but her underwear, she anticipated feeling his hands on her frame. She almost felt bad, as she and Kevin had barely kissed, and he had only seen her legs in a pair of shorts a few times. Then she remembered how it semed like lately he wanted nothing to do with her, so she put the guilt aside and hopped her mostly naked body under the crisp white sheet and thick blanket.

After a few minutes, a she heard a light knock on the door. "You ready?" Dexter asked.

Was she? "Yes, you can come in."

Dexter entered the room. The spice from his cologne tickled her nose, among other things. Ava was thankful she was facing down first. She didn't need to see him again just yet. Her senses were already heightened. He folded the top of the blanket that covered her back down to the top of her behind.

His hands were warm and slippery with a scented oil as he caressed her back. Ava appreciated his large, soothing hands. Her stresses floated away with every stroke. She should've done this a long time ago.

"Is the pressure okay?"

"Yes, it's perfect." She didn't mean to sound so turned on. *Well, too late now.*

"Good." He continued to do everything right from head to toe.

He had unusually soft hands for a man. They did their job, making Ava so relaxed that she nodded off a few times. When it came time for her to flip over, she looked forward to sneaking a peek as he worked. Dexter lifted the sheet toward him to cover his view, but at that point, Ava didn't care if he saw anything.

"Are you doing all right?" He covered her body and ran his hand smoothly over her entire body, sending a tingle down her spine.

"Yes, I am. Thank you."

This time, he started from the bottom and worked his way up. When he reached her inner thigh, she jerked.

"Is everything okay?" He paused in his movement.

"Yes, I'm fine. Probably too fine." Ava chuckled. "I'm trying not to enjoy it too much."

He leaned in closer to her ear. "You can enjoy it as much you want." His warm breath, mixed together with the cologne, was too much. He returned to her leg and continued applying just the right amount of pressure.

Somewhere in the middle of calming the fibers in her body and turning her on, she moaned. "I'm sorry. I'm not trying to move around."

"It's quite all right. And I'm serious. We can take this as far as you want to. It'll just be between us."

What exactly was he offering? And the more important question was, did she want to take him up on his offer? She wasn't tied down anymore. Ava was in another country, and no one ever had to find out. She could keep this to herself, and her mind definitely wouldn't be on Kevin anymore. Why shouldn't she indulge?

Surely, Dexter had played this game with several tourists before her. She didn't need to know, but her curiosity spoke for her. "What exactly do you mean?"

"I can show you better than I can tell you. Just let me know if you want me to stop."

"Okay." She spoke against the last little moral bone in her body that screamed for him to stop.

He hovered over her and lowered his face over her mouth. When his lips touched hers, an electric shock traveled through her body. The sensuality of the spontaneous scene called her name for more. Dexter's hands explored her body, and although she knew she shouldn't engage in that type of behavior, she couldn't stop. Her body wouldn't let her even if she tried. She had fallen for the enemy. For the moment.

This handsome man wanted her, so she dove in. He would need to provide the life jacket, though, if they did end up going too far. She wasn't prepared for this type of fantasy turning into a reality, but she welcomed it all the same. It felt good to her to be wanted, even if she wasn't his first or last. For the moment, it was more than okay with her.

Chapter Twenty-four

The next morning, Ava's regret filled up her hotel room. What had she done? Was she really feeling that low where she chose to have sex with a man she'd just met or didn't even care for? She needed to grow up. Just because something wasn't going her way didn't mean she had to react the way she always did. It was a major sign of her spiritual immaturity. Her vices were alcohol and sex, and when her world fell apart, one way or another, she always found her way back to both.

That could be why the Lord had kept marriage out of her reach, to protect herself and her future husband. If she continued to behave like this, she may never be ready to walk down that aisle. She shifted her focus for a few moments, and now she was back to where she started: feeling sorry and disgusted.

Her cell phone buzzed. Rene was probably calling to let her know what time to meet in her room. When Ava saw Kevin's picture on her screen, her stomach twisted into knots.

"Hello?" She tried to sound as normal as possible.

"Hey, Ava. Good to hear your voice."

"Yours too." *Wish you would've called a lot sooner.* But he was on the phone now, so she should just take advantage of the opportunity and not complain. "I've missed you."

"And I've missed you too." He paused and cleared his throat. "Sorry I haven't called. I've been quite busy with all that's going on."

"It's okay, I understand." *For the most part, I guess.* "How is everything?"

"Well, I'd like to meet you somewhere. We've had something tragic happen in the family, and I think seeing your smile would help me a great deal."

How guilty did she feel now? "Well, I'm actually in Jamaica, so I can't meet you, but we can talk as long as you need to."

"In Jamaica? So I don't talk to you for a few days and you leave the country on me, huh?" His caring disposition, with a hint of jealousy, was sweet.

Ava giggled. "Yep, well, it happens. Wish you could've made the trip with me." She wished that more than anything right then.

"Was there a special occasion, or just a getaway with the girls?"

She enjoyed his sincere interest. "Rene's getting married."

"Dang, I guess I missed a lot."

That'll teach him to push me aside. "Yes, you have."

"I wish I could be there with you, but with what's going on, I probably wouldn't have been able to make the trip anyway."

"You're scaring me, Kevin. What's going on?"

"Well, Tweet finally called me after she snuck out of the rehab facility. She wanted me to come get her from a dangerous part of downtown."

"Mmm. Is she okay now?"

Ava could only hear sniffles.

"Kevin, what's the matter? Did something happen to Tweet? Kevin, talk to me."

"Ah, Ava." He took in a deep breath and followed with another sniffle. "She's gone. By the time I got to her, she'd already been shot. She died right there in my arms."

"Oh, no, Kevin. I'm so sorry. I wish I were there with you." Ava would give anything to be able to put her arms around him and hold on with a firm, loving grip until he got tired.

"Thank you, but I'm worried about my mother. She's not taking it so well." He coughed. "Yeah, she learned at her last doctor's appointment a week or so ago that her blood pressure is sky high. The doctors were surprised she hadn't had a stroke."

Even though Ava didn't care for Gladys, she wouldn't wish the pain of losing a child on anyone. Nor would she want anyone to go through health scares. Navigating through life was hard enough without being sick.

Ava could hear the tension in his voice as he spoke in a dry tone. "And I'm trying to plan Tweet's funeral, so I really haven't had time to process all of this."

"Do you want me to fly home tonight and help you out?"

"No, it's okay. I don't want you to miss your best friend's wedding. I've set the viewing for Tuesday evening, and the funeral will be on Wednesday at two. When are you coming back?"

"I'll be home tomorrow. I can come straight to you and help you with whatever you need." She was eager to get by his side.

"That would be great. I could really use you here, Ava. I'm so sorry for ending things. I miss your friendship, and really need you in my life right now and always."

"Kevin, I'm sorry too. I should have never made you choose between your family and me. It will never be like that moving forward. I want you back in my life. No matter how much your family disapproves of me. I'm still there for you. I will see you soon. Kevin?"

"Yes, Ava, I'm still here."

"I love you unconditionally."

"I feel the same, Ava. I will see you soon." He hung up the phone.

Ava was sorry for her part in their breakup and so much more. From the ultimatum to the sex with a stranger, did she want to sabotage the best thing in her life? How could she be so stupid? She was willing to risk her relationship, rocky or not, for a sinful act of passion. The man she loved needed her, while she was busy feeding her insecurities. Had she learned nothing from her mistakes with Rene and Ishmael? Wasn't that enough of a wakeup call to her misguided actions?

Ava needed to put the situation aside for the moment and focus on her best friend and her wedding day, but could she really do that? Could she put on the fake smile and go through with everything as if she didn't care?

Once she entered Rene's suite and laid her eyes on her dress and her smile, Ava was able to envelop herself into Rene's world. Her mother was busy fanning her underarms, which made the girls giggle when their eyes met. Ava remembered back to her middle school days, when she and Rene would daydream about their wedding day, lying across one of their beds; and now she was getting ready to be a part of Rene's dream come true.

Ava looked forward to the day that Rene would return the favor and stand by her side as she one day wed Kevin. If her dream came true as well, Ava was ready. She had it all planned out. All Kevin would have to do was make sure he and his family showed up at the right place and on time.

"Girl, you are absolutely beautiful." Ava hugged Rene, keeping their faces from touching to make sure their makeup stayed intact. Rene didn't have her lawyer hat on at all. In fact, she looked as if she worked with Toni on the runway. She could've jumped off the pages of a wedding catalogue.

"Thank you, Ava. You look beautiful too." Rene beamed. Ava hadn't seen her that happy in a long time.

She bounced up and down, holding her hands together. "I can't believe this day is here."

"I can. And you deserve it, girl. Paul is the perfect man for you, and I know he will make you happy. God has hooked both of you up. Your life together will be amazing."

Rene's eyes started to fill with tears. "Nope, I can't mess up my makeup."

Ava snatched a couple of tissues and dabbed Rene's eyes. The two finished the final preparations and then toasted with a glass of champagne with Rene's mother.

I should never have another drink as long as I live. But if she didn't take at least a sip, Rene would wonder why, and then Ava would have to spill the jacked-up beans.

This time at the wedding, Ava wouldn't pick apart what she would do differently. She would just support her friend and enjoy the moment. Her brother, Alex, was the best man, of course, so it was a family affair. They would have a fun time as two of their closest friends in the world got hitched. It had to be a God-ordained union.

Even though she took pleasure in the festivities, Ava's guilt and shame of what she had done the night before loomed over her like a dark cloud. What did the forecast hold in her future: God-ordained union, or colossal mistake that caused her to forever be alone? She was battling the conversations in her mind as to how stupid she was and how she could let alcohol take over.

Chapter Twenty-five

When Ava arrived back at her domain, she could hardly wait to contact Kevin to help him finalize the plans for Tweet's funeral. She wanted to be his biggest source of support and comfort.

As she went to reach for her phone, her ringtone went off. "Hello," she answered.

"Hi, Ms. Alexander, please." The woman's voice on the other end of the line was very professional.

"This is she."

"Hello. My name is Carla Turner, and I'm calling from Bank of Texas. I have some great news for you."

"I'm listening. I'm always ready to hear some good news."

"A couple of weeks ago, you applied for a business loan, and I know it didn't go through for you, but Johnny, your loan officer, passed your information on to me. After gathering a few more documents and information, I was able to get you approved through this new government program designed to help small businesses get started."

"Glory to God. That's awesome." Yep, the Lord was showing out. He loved her unconditionally and continued to bless her in spite of herself.

"We just need to schedule a time when you can come and go over all the documents and sign them."

She needed to keep her next few days free to be able to commit that time to Kevin. "I'm available Thursday any time."

"Sounds good. How about at nine a.m. here at my office?"

"I'll be there." Her dream was now in motion.

"Okay, great. Between now and then, if you have the time, feel free to check out a few spaces you may want to lease for your restaurant. Write the addresses down, and I'll have the Realtor we use get with you on that. And congratulations to you, Ms. Alexander."

"Thank you so much."

What was God up to? Within the last twenty-four hours, he'd ushered Kevin back into her life and had given her a business loan to be able to make her restaurant dream come true. Whatever His plan was, she was down with it. Ava found Kevin's name in her contact numbers and pushed the SEND icon.

"Hey, babe."

"Hey, Kev. How are you doing?" She loved hearing his voice. Even with a hint of sadness added, his voice still pulled her into whatever he was saying at the time.

"As good as I can right about now. Trying to stay busy."

"Yeah, I bet. Well, I'm home now, and I'm all yours." Ava truly meant the last words she spoke. She was all his and wanted everyone to know it. "Just let me know what you want me to do."

"I'd love it if you could come over to my mom's house."

"Your mom's house?" Ava wanted to be there for him, but she wasn't prepared to enter his mother's house again just yet. During her last visit, things didn't go so well. She didn't want to revisit that atmosphere again.

"Yes, I've been staying here since Tweet died, and planning her funeral from here." He sighed. "I know what you're thinking, and it'll be fine."

"I appreciate that, but I don't want to add any stress to what you're already going through, and I feel like the tension between me and your family would do just that." Was she letting him down again?

Kevin took a deep breath. "Don't worry about my mom and sisters. I love you, and they need to be happy that I'm happy. So it shouldn't be a problem. I promise."

"I love you too and want to be there for you, but I don't need any drama."

"If there's drama, I'll handle it. I need you here with me."

That's all Ava needed to hear. "I'll be there as soon as I can. I'm opening the car door as we speak. See you soon."

As Kevin cleaned the oven, he still couldn't shake thoughts of his baby sister being gone. No amount of housework could get his mind off of his current situation. It was essential that he sit down at some point to write Tweet's eulogy, but he procrastinated, finding other activities to delay him from expressing his feelings about his sister's life. Many only knew her as a drug addict, so the task at hand was a difficult one.

It was good to hear Ava's voice, and he couldn't wait to put his arms around her for some much-needed comfort. Her presence wouldn't make the pain of the loss go away, nothing would, but his soul could stand to see the warm smile he'd missed. Her being there would make everything easier. His mom and sisters would just have to deal with her presence.

Thirty minutes passed and the doorbell rang.

"Kevin? Who could that be?" His sister Martha marched toward the door.

Kevin stopped her as she reached the door. "It's for me, Martha. Let me open the door. You can go back to Momma's side."

She lingered back a bit, hoping to see their visitor, but he didn't open the door until she was out of the room. Kevin didn't want Martha to spill any bad comments out of her mouth to make Ava turn her back once again.

Kevin's heart fluttered as he opened the door and welcomed Ava into his arms. Tears escaped his eyes. He didn't necessarily want her to see him cry, but with the situation at hand, tears were inevitable. Being in her arms felt like home. He didn't want to let her go. Ever again.

"I'm so sorry, Kevin." Her eyes offered the light he needed.

"Thank you for being here, Ava. I've missed you."

She smiled. "I've missed you too. You can't even imagine how much."

He suspected it was about as much as he'd missed her. Kevin would have liked to go back and change his decision to break things off with her. Ultimatum or no ultimatum, his pride had driven him to that choice, and he wouldn't let that happen again. They had lost valuable time together, but she was back in his life now, so he treasured that.

Holding on to him tightly, she asked, "What do you need me to do?"

"Basically, all the plans are done." Kevin stepped back and rubbed his eyes. "The services are set. I just need to write the eulogy, but I don't know where to start." He ushered her over to the living space.

"Well, I can help you with that." Ava grabbed the notepad and pen that he had placed on the coffee table a few attempts ago. She sat on the couch and patted the cushion next to her. "Come have a seat, baby. Let's get started."

Her calm spirit put him at ease. Yep, he was definitely glad she was there. He took the seat next to her, scooting as close to her as physically possible. "What do you suggest I write about?"

"Well, you can always start from the beginning. Talk about your relationship when y'all were little kids, and go from there. You were always close, right?"

"Yes, we were." He smirked as he pictured Tweet's face. She nodded. "Then talk about that."

"But I can't help but think that we were so close that I was the one to introduce her to this destructive drug path she was on. And I couldn't help her."

"There were many others aspects to your relationship besides that, I'm sure. Focus on the positive." Ava handed him the pad and pen. "What were her best qualities? What did you guys do together? What was her favorite game to play with you?"

Tweet had released him from being responsible for her choice of drug addiction, yet he still felt he pointed her in that direction, and that guilt would never leave. Still, Ava was right. He didn't have to focus on that. Her life offered so much more, and he could talk about that.

Lord, help me to write the perfect words that represent my baby sister's life. I need your help. Holy Spirit, take over and write it for me.

"What is she doing here?" Kevin's mother's voice broke up his silent prayer. She walked into the room with his sisters. "I knew I heard an unwelcome voice."

Kevin put his hand in the air. "Momma, don't start. It's not the time."

"Kevin Jacob Allen, we are mourning your sister's death." Gladys threw her tissues down in disgust. "This is our business, and whosoever is not a part of this family should leave. Now!" Her eyes turned to Ava.

Martha added her two cents. "Yeah, Kev, I thought you were done with that chick. I thought she was making you choose your family or her."

Ava sat up, about to stand.

Kevin placed his hand on her leg. "No, Ava, you don't have to go anywhere." He stood and walked over to his family. "Yes, Momma, I know very well that we are mourning Tweet's death. Ava is helping me write the eulogy."

Mary smacked her lips and then said, "She didn't know Tweet like that to help with something so important. Why don't you go to the flower shop and get another vase of flowers."

"Mary, be careful here. Maybe she didn't know Tweet like we did, but she's the only one here who offered to help me out. You all just expect me to do everything and haven't offered a hand with anything." Kevin sauntered over to Ava and grabbed her hand to stand up.

His mother scoffed. "Well, I told you that it hurts too much to make these decisions about her funeral or I would help. Ava can't be that much help anyway."

"I'm serious, Momma. If you all want to continue to treat Ava this way, I don't have to come by here anymore, and you'll lose a son, too." He cocked his neck and pursed his lips, waiting for anyone to say something smart. The blank expressions on their faces were enough for him. "That's what I thought."

He handed Ava the pad and pen and then grabbed his keys.

"Kevin, where are you going?" His mother's voice cracked with worry.

"Ava and I will finish this elsewhere. I'll see y'all at the viewing tomorrow night. If you even know where it is."

After he slammed the door behind them, he looked into Ava's eyes. She rubbed his back in support as they walked to her car. Seeing her smile was all he needed. He hadn't felt a peace like that in weeks, and he wanted to hold on to that for the rest of his life. He was more than happy to have her back in his life.

Chapter Twenty-six

After leaving Gladys's house in the abrupt way they did, Ava helped Kevin finish scripting the eulogy at her house, where he was always welcome. Then later that night, after reading it through a couple of times out loud to Ava, he returned to his house, instead of going back to his mother's house. Ava knew he needed to calm himself down before he returned to the house he grew up in. Although she wanted him to spend the night, she knew he also needed his space to mourn.

Tweet's viewing was held the next evening at their family's church. Ava gave her support, not saying anything to anyone in Kevin's immediate family, but remaining by his side when she arrived. It was definitely a downer for Ava. As much as she wanted to smile and hug Kevin for returning to her, she couldn't. Ava offered to go back to his house with him, but he politely declined and went to his mother's instead. He probably thought it would be best if she wasn't there.

Afterward, she looked forward to catching up with her girls over dinner. They hadn't seen each other since the wedding. She sat sipping her glass of water as she awaited their arrival. Her excitement about her new business venture bubbled over. She'd probably burst out with it as soon as they both got to her table at one of her favorite restaurants.

Rene and Toni must've pulled up at the same time, because they came strolling into the restaurant together.

Ava wasn't sure which glow was most prominent: that of the newlywed or the mother-to-be. Ava jumped to her feet to hug the ladies. Glory wasn't able to make it, as she had a commitment with Greg's family, which was good for her and Greg's relationship, Ava was certain. She could fill Glory in later.

"Between this newlywed glow and the pregnant woman glow shining from you two, I do believe I need to put my shades on." Ava giggled.

"Well, you know. I'm loving married life." Rene got situated in her seat. "I know it hasn't been a full week yet, but I'm loving it all the same."

Toni grinned. "I bet you're getting all you can, huh?"

"Yes, I am." Rene couldn't contain her smile. "And the best part is, it's with my husband. I am having guilt-free sex with the man I love. Doesn't get any better than that." She looked at Ava. "Sorry, girl. I know you and Kevin are waiting. Not trying to throw it in your face."

"It's quite all right." Ava looked down at her hands. "Matter of fact, I haven't been very good at the waiting part."

"You and Kevin got down?" Toni's eyes were wide.

"Nope, he's fine. You know me and how I work."

Rene stared at her. "Yeah, but you've changed." Rene threw a confused look to Toni.

"Not as much as I thought." Ava hesitated, trying to decide if she really wanted to tell on herself. She knew she had to take a deep breath before revealing anything. "When we were in Jamaica, the night before the wedding, I was in one of my moods behind my breakup with Kevin, and you know I'd been drinking. I ended up putting myself in a tempting situation."

Toni scolded her. "Ava, what did you do?"

Shaking her head, she looked at Toni and said, "Well, I told you I was going to get a massage, right?"

"Yes." Toni sat back in her chair, putting her arms on the side as if to brace herself for the news.

Ava closed her eyes, as if what she did would magically go away with the blink of her eyes like a genie. "Well, the masseur and I went way past the massage. I'm sure we broke a long list of the company's rules."

"How could you, Ava?" Rene was now the scolder. "What about Kevin? I thought you were ready to either let go or find a resolution, especially after our weekend trip."

"Kevin is Kevin. We weren't together, and—"

"Are you going to tell him?" Toni's eyes squinted as she tilted her head. Ava felt the fire of disapproval shoot from her eyes.

"No, I'm not planning on it. I know I messed up and should've handled my emotions in a healthier fashion, but I didn't, and there's no need to create drama where there isn't any." *What he doesn't know won't hurt him.*

"Ava, you've got to get control of your emotions and your actions behind your emotions." Toni's eyes were sad. "I'm afraid if you keep behavior like this up, God may never want to give you your heart's desire by way of a husband. Because when you're mad at him for one thing or another, and you will get mad from time to time, you can't react this way. It doesn't work like that, Ava."

Rene's eyes read the same disapproval. "Ava, you have to handle your feelings in a more mature manner. This is no way to act. I'm surprised at you, Ava."

"I know." Ava tried not to sound like she had an attitude. "And I've said all this to myself and to God. I don't know what's wrong with me. I guess I can't handle my emotions."

Toni grabbed her hand. "Nothing's wrong with you. You're human, and we all make mistakes and poor choices. We just have to learn from them, move on, and do our best not to make the same mistakes over and over again." She glanced at Rene.

"We love you and believe in you, Ava." Rene leaned in and placed her hand over Ava's other hand. "But you've got to believe in yourself. Here God has brought this wonderful man into your life, and you don't want to mess that up with being childish and messy."

"Yep, he's my DC." Ava gave a nervous giggle. "And I've been waiting for him. I've got to do better. I believe I can do better with him back in my life."

"Remember, you can still do better with him out of your life." Rene raised her glass to toast.

Toni sat back in her seat, thinking about Ava's comment. "Your DC? What's that? I've never heard of that term before. Is it a young thing?"

Ava reached out for her glass of water again. "My dangling carrot."

"Explain." Rene giggled, shaking her head.

"I feel like God is holding Kevin, this awesome godly man, in front of me. If I can just do right, he could be what I have been searching for all my life; but when he dropped me with the quickness after I gave him the ultimatum, I was hoping that God wouldn't dangle this wonderful man in front of me only to take him away. Therefore, he's my dangling carrot."

Toni laughed. "That's cute. Remember, you need to do right to get the prize, just like the rabbit when they dangle the carrot in front of him. *Do right* being the key phrase."

Ava understood and would go to God in prayer before ever making another poor choice where a man was concerned. Hopefully, Kevin was it for her, and she wouldn't put herself in any more tempting situations that would threaten the successful prize of her DC. "I do have some good news to share."

"Hurry and spill it before this becomes a 'bring Ava to her senses' intervention." Toni slapped the table.

"Well, I received a call from the bank where I applied for my small business loan, and apparently there is this new government program that helps small businesses get started." She put her glass back down and pointed her thumbs at herself. "I have been approved for the loan."

"Oh, Ava. I'm so happy for you." Rene stood up out of her chair to lean over and give her a hug. "I know you've been waiting on this dream for a long time."

"Congratulations, girl. So where is it going to be?" Toni wanted more details.

"Not sure yet. I'm supposed to be looking at locations before Thursday, when I go in to sign the paperwork."

"Ooh, ooh." Rene bounced in her seat, clapping her hands. "Say no more. I have the perfect spot. And the best part is it's right next to my law office."

"Are you serious?"

"As a heart attack. The current tenant is in the process of moving out as we speak. It was a sandwich shop, so it's already set up to serve hungry customers. We gotta go see it first thing tomorrow."

"I'm down with that." Toni clapped.

Ava's heart overflowed with joy. Everything was happening in God's timing. Could she just stay on board with what He wanted instead of what she wanted? Then it would work out for her best anyway.

"So how are you and the baby doing, Toni?" Ava didn't want to take up the whole conversation with her life's situations.

"Well, he and I are doing just fine."

"He?" Ava and Rene questioned together.

Toni cheesed from one ear to the other. "Yes, it's a boy! We just found out a few days ago."

The trio's screams alerted others in the establishment of the good news. After they hugged Toni and quieted down, they were able to regain focus.

"So, I know Eric is happy he's gonna have a little version of himself running around here." Ava pictured the toddler looking just like Eric. No doubt he'd be a handsome child with Toni and Eric for parents.

"Yes, he is quite excited." Toni chuckled. "He already bought him a Dallas Cowboys onesie."

Rene shook her head. "Have y'all picked out a name yet?"

"Eric Anthony III is the best we can come up with. I know it makes Eric proud to keep his family name going, so I'm all for it."

"That's cool. I am so happy for the both of you." Ava recognized all the good that was going on in the lives of her girlfriends and was grateful.

"With all this great news, I hate to bring this up, but I do want to fill you in on what's going on with me and Kevin." She didn't want to be a downer, but her girls needed to know one more aspect of her and Kevin's relationship. "I did want to let you guys know that Kevin and I are talking again, but it was tragedy that brought us together, so please keep him and his family in prayer."

"Oh, no. What happened?" Toni clutched her chest.

"His baby sister, Tweet, was shot and killed. It was some sort of drug deal gone wrong." Ava's bottom lip turned up. "I've been doing what I can to help him, not that his family has been any help. But we are talking again."

"Girl, why didn't you tell us when we first got here?" Toni sat back and put her hand on her hip.

"I know." Ava shook her head. "I just wanted to wait for the right time to slide the news in, and I wanted to hear about you guys first."

"Well, I hate it took this to get you two together again, but I know he appreciates having you there by his side at this time," Rene assured her.

"And he would be the only one. His mom and sisters still have an attitude toward me, but this time I think he shut them up for good."

"That sounds promising." Toni gave her a thumbs-up.

"Yeah, well, we'll see." Ava knew her girls supported her no matter what. She also knew that God would guide her down the right path where everything in her life was concerned.

What she did not know was what would truly become of her and Kevin's relationship, but she was confident in the one who did know. The Lord would work things out for her good, and that was all she needed to know.

Chapter Twenty-seven

The inside of the sanctuary, solemn in spirit, was quiet with the exception of people saying hello to one another at their arrival. Ava sat at the end of the aisle. She positioned herself close to the front, where she believed Kevin would be, yet she was out of the direct circle of family who would enter and sit in the first couple of rows.

The pastor asked everyone to stand as the immediate family slumped through the doors of the church. Kevin, carrying a tissue, held his mother's hand. So, at least in that moment, the strife between them had ceased. Ava felt for her man. Nothing would bring Tweet back; however, that was the only thing that would lift Kevin's spirit. She felt helpless. The love of Ava's life was hurting, and there was nothing she could do except be there for him. Hopefully, that would be enough.

As Kevin and his family walked down the center aisle to the front, Ava couldn't help herself. Her beau, dressed to the nines, had her undivided attention. He wore sadness on his face, but her attraction to him wouldn't turn off just because of the situation. Kevin was a good-looking man, and no circumstance could get in the way of Ava seeing that.

Focus, girl.

After the family settled in their seats, the pastor delivered a powerful opening prayer. Certain words pulled at Ava's soul. Words like "forgiveness," "unconditional love," and "opportunities and open doors." By the time the pastor completed his prayer, Ava was ready to head to the altar.

An unplanned pause occurred in the ceremony as Mary, Kevin's sister, struggled to get out of her seat. Her tears and pain were evident. She seemed to will through as Kevin escorted her to the front. She crept to the microphone and podium next to the gray-and-black casket. She took a second to get her bearings then looked at the pianist and nodded. Her rendition of "Walk Around Heaven" brought tears to Ava's eyes. When the last lyrics of the song were voiced, sniffles filled the room. Mary's voice shook, but her professional-sounding tone blew Ava away.

His sister possessed a talent Ava never knew she had. Ava didn't know much about his sisters, because they seemed to prefer it that way. Maybe one day the dynamic between them would change, but for now, she'd just have to learn things on her own as they came. Ava had done all she'd known to try to foster a relationship, but she was tired of making all the effort, and she would let it just play out on its own. The only fact she did know was his family wouldn't be able to treat her just any old way. Kevin would make sure of that. Then, maybe, they'd get the idea that she didn't plan on going anywhere, and they'd leave her be.

Ava refocused her attention on Kevin as he got up to help Mary return to her seat. Then he strolled his fine frame behind the podium. He covered his mouth as he cleared his throat and then reached into the inside of his jacket pocket. Pulling out his eulogy, Kevin took a deep breath and then slowly unfolded the paper.

"Kaleeya Lashaun Allen, or Tweet, as the family called her, left this earth way too soon. Growing up, she would always talk about her hopes and dreams, and although she didn't get the chance to leave her mark in this world the way she wanted to, she did leave us with a few lessons." He paused to wipe a tear from his eye. "Tweet truly cared about other people and treated everyone with respect, no matter their background or circumstance. Especially outsiders. She could make everyone in the room feel comfortable and important."

Proud of her man and the loving words he spoke, Ava smiled on the inside. He spoke with sincerity and a calm confidence. She loved him for so many things. The relationship he had shared with his baby sister and how he loved her unconditionally was one of the items on Ava's list of things to love about Kevin.

He looked up from his paper to glance at his mother and sisters sitting in the front row. "I believe her addiction was a cry for help. She was just never able to kick the habit for good. But now she's in God's hands, and He's taking care of her. She will be missed, thought about often, and always loved." His voice cracked as he dabbed his eyes. "And, Tweet, I just want to say . . ." He breathed heavy. "I just want to say . . ."

"It's all right, Kevin. Let it out, brotha," the pastor shouted from behind him.

"I just want to say, I'm sorry. I wish I could've been the big brother you needed me to be." His hands clasped the podium as he couldn't hold it in any longer. "Oh, God, why did you have to take her so soon? She still had life to live on this earth." His tears became an all-out yelp and spastic cry.

Ava immediately got up from her seat to go be with him. She wanted nothing more than to take his pain away. Throwing her arms around him tightly would have to be enough; it was all she could do at that moment. Kevin turned to her and wrapped his arms around her body. She was happy to be at the altar in support of her man, and she'd stay there as long as he needed her to.

***

As people set plates of food down on Kevin's mother's dining room table, Kevin just watched. He'd have rather been home alone with his thoughts and memories of Tweet. How was he going to go on without his baby sister? Was he ever going to be the same?

As he stood there in the dining room, sipping the sweet punch, Kevin saw Mike, one of his clients, staring at him out of the corner of his eye. He remembered the last time they really spoke, he helped Mike dispose of a bag of cocaine he'd been carrying around. After knocking temptation in the face that day, Kevin hadn't seen him much. He question Mike's motives. Yeah, he knew him, but not that well. Hopefully, he wasn't there to present the temptation again. The tragic situation might help to steer him in the wrong direction.

Kevin turned to head in the opposite direction and Mike seemed to bolt after him.

Mike reached out to give Kevin a hug. "Hey, Kevin. I heard about your sister, and I had to come and show my love and support."

Kevin returned the gesture and then stepped back. "I appreciate you, man. And my family does too."

"This would be a good time for you to take a hit of a little somethin' somethin'." He touched Kevin on the shoulder, not wasting any time getting to his real reason for showing up. "Everyone will understand, and if they don't, so what? It's your life, not theirs."

Kevin couldn't act like the thought hadn't crossed his mind; but he had come so far, staying clean for the past eleven . He couldn't allow his heartbreak behind his sister's death to open up that can of worms. "Naw, man. I can't get down like that anymore. Plus, I'm supposed to be helping you, remember?"

Mike laughed. "Yeah, I remember."

"Where've you been lately?"

"Well, you know. I've been around. And I was just joking, but you seem like you were really considering it. I don't mean to be a pusher or anything, but you just lost your sister. Nobody would fault you if you took a hit or two." He was delivering his speech like a used car salesman. "And it would help you forget about the pain for a couple of hours."

Kevin shook his head, but his mind started turning, thinking of ways he could use without anyone finding out. "Yeah, I lost my sister behind that stuff, and I don't want to cloud my memory of everything that's going on."

"Well, you got my number. I can get some and be at your house a little later if you want me to." He saluted him as he started backing up. "Just let me know. I'm here for you, brotha."

Mike was out the door that quick. It was like the enemy just sent him in for that one play of the game. Kevin would do his best to avoid that challenge altogether. Mike, no doubt, saw his offer as helping a friend through a tough time, but that was not the type of "here for you, brotha" help Kevin was in need of.

The thought did roll around in his brain, though, and he wasn't sure what to do with it. He could explain to Ava and his family that he just wanted to be alone that night. They would understand. But God wouldn't. He would know his motives.

After the family's supporters stayed a couple of hours, ate plates of food, and made sure the family had everything they needed, folks started to head out. Kevin was glad to see people go as he thought more and more about Mike's proposal. He knew nothing would bring Tweet back, but he couldn't ignore the desire he had to use again. The craving was evident and not going anywhere.

Kevin lounged on the couch for about a half hour after the last guest left the house. While looking through the TV past whatever show was on, he went back and forth, toying with the idea of snorting cocaine again. Was he really considering it? He wasn't sure that using would help him any, but he was willing to try. But how could he? Kevin was a drug counselor. He was supposed to point others in the direction away from drugs, yet here he was ready to pick up the phone and call his contact.

He left his mother's house with a heavy heart, missing his sister and needing to use again. Kevin thought the drive to his house would shake his temptations.

After a few more *yes*es than *no*s in his head, he went on with his plan. Putting everything and everyone else aside that evening, he thought of himself only. He walked into his house and walked straight to his bedroom. He removed his suit and put on a pair of sweatpants and a T-shirt. Kevin lay across his bed, hoping he would somehow fall asleep and his feeling of temptation would disappear.

He tossed and turned for about an hour then he suddenly stood up and paced the floor. His mind wanted to feel that great feeling of nothing again. No worries. No heartaches. No sadness.

Kevin searched for his cell phone. He held it in his hand, contemplating again. Should he? Would he feel better? Would it bring him the satisfaction he needed at the moment? He stared at his phone as if it would send him a sign of what to do. He waited and stared for a good ten minutes, but nothing happened. His urge to be relieved of everything for just a few hours was turning into self-satisfaction.

He dialed Mike without any more hesitation. He was convinced that there was only one way for his urges to subside: just do it one last time. Was that really the best way? Why didn't he pray? Call someone? Anything but this.

"Yo, who this?"

"It's Kevin. You still got that for me?" He hated the way those words sounded out loud.

"Yeah, man. I got you. I'll be over there in no time at all."

As soon as Kevin hung up the phone, he was filled with guilt. How could he destroy all his hard work for the past eleven ? His own sister died because of her addiction. Would this open a door he had closed long ago? Kevin sat on the bed, thinking he may have just made one of the biggest mistakes of his life.

The doorbell rang suddenly, shaking Kevin out of his thoughts. First he thought of not answering the door. Then the bell sounded again. He slowly went to open the door. It was less than twenty minutes ago that they'd talked. Mike made it to his house in record time.

As Kevin opened the door, Mike seemed all too eager to jump at the chance to have a new drug buddy. Was Kevin really about to erase his eleven of sobriety? He was stronger than that. Or so he thought.

Mike hurried in and sat down on the sofa then presented Kevin with the plastic bag filled with the white powdery substance. Kevin retrieved a small plate from his kitchen cabinet and handed it to Mike for him to prepare the sinfest that was about to take place. It was too late to turn back now. The routine of getting everything set up was something Kevin hadn't forgotten. It was like riding a bike. He knew if he did indulge, he wouldn't be worried about any bikes, but more like kites, as he'd be as high as one.

A bit nervous about how he might react after snorting the substance he had grown to love so many years ago,

Kevin hesitated. He wanted to speak up to Mike about removing himself and his cocaine from his house, but after seeing Mike carefully make the perfect lines on the plate, his mouth watered, anticipating his first inhale.

After all prep work was done, Mike handed Kevin a rolled-up dollar bill and said, "Your sister's funeral. You get to do the honors."

As Kevin grabbed the bill from Mike's hand, everything in his mind screamed, *Stop! Don't do it!* But with the first snort of the first line, he quickly quieted those voices. What had he done? What if the people at the Christian Counseling Center could see him now? His family? The love of his life? How was he honoring the memory of his sister? That was just it. He wasn't. After inhaling his third line of coke, he didn't care how anyone felt.

Chapter Twenty-eight

That Sunday morning, Ava waited patiently for Kevin to show up at her apartment. She hadn't seen him since the funeral. She wanted to give him his space to grieve. He knew she would be there when he needed her. So besides a couple of brief phone conversations and a few texts, they hadn't really spoken that much over the past three days.

But now, Kevin was headed to pick her up so they could travel to church together. He was running late, which was very unlike him. She was unsure what sort of mental and emotional state he was in; yet she would support him regardless. Ava loved him with all of her heart. When he hurt, she hurt. She'd do her best to help alleviate some of the pain if she could. She couldn't wait to feel him in her arms.

Ava's worry led her to pick up her cell and check on where he was. As she was about to hit the SEND button after dialing his phone number, there was a knock at the door. Ava hustled over to answer it.

With the door only partially open, Kevin busted through and pulled her close to him. "Ah, Ava. It's so good to see you." He held on tight.

"Good to see you too, babe." She sensed something wasn't right with him. "Is everything okay?"

Still holding her, he said, "Actually, no." It was killing him to tell the love of his life that he took a turn off the straight path, but he knew he had to in order to move forward and truly give Ava the choice of staying with him or not. He hated to believe that he may just lose the love of his life over his selfishness.

She stepped back to look in his eyes. "What's the matter, Kevin?"

"I have seriously messed up. I really don't know how to explain myself other than my weakness took a hold of me in the worst way. "

"How, babe? You're scaring me." Did he do the unthinkable? Was there someone else? Did he make the same mistake she had, and now coming clean would be the only righteous thing to do? Ava braced herself for the worst.

He held his hand over his mouth as if he wanted to keep the words in a bit longer. "The other night after the funeral, I gave in to temptation."

Fear that the bottom was about to drop out, Ava steadied herself. "What happened, Kevin? Just say it, please."

Kevin shook his head. "This guy I counsel at the center is a recent recovering addict. Well, he was a recovering addict. He came to the funeral and offered me a way to forget about everything for the moment." He swallowed hard. "And I took him up on it."

"You used drugs with a patient of yours?" Hoping she didn't sound too judgmental, Ava wasn't prepared to deal with that situation. Sure, she had hit a little weed in college, but she had never gotten hooked on anything and didn't understand how the addict's mind worked.

Kevin nervously chuckled. "Trust me, it surprised me as well. I needed to forget everything just for a short time. I know that's no excuse. No matter how I say it, I can't make it sound even halfway right. I seriously can't believe I did that after eleven years of sobriety. I let my pain of losing Tweet rule everything else."

"So that's why I haven't seen you much the past few days?" She caressed his face.

He held his head down. "Yep, I was definitely too ashamed. But I had to see you, and I need to go to church."

"Well, how'd you feel? You didn't do anything crazy, did you?"

He shrugged his shoulders. "Not sure I can explain it, but it wasn't the same. Good news is I couldn't even enjoy the high. I wasn't in a good place, and the coke didn't help one bit. I need to remember that feeling." Kevin shook his head as he spoke. "Yep, I need remember that I didn't enjoy it, so that I won't be so quick to let history repeat itself."

"I'm sure you won't forget, but most importantly, remember God does forget. Once you've asked for forgiveness, believe you have received it and move on." Ava needed to remind herself of that very fact from time to time.

As they headed out the door, elation set in, as she was glad to be back by his side and attending church services with him. Being together in the house of the Lord, fostering their spiritual bond, was important to Ava. How a man managed and lived his spiritual life had always been a big check-off for Ava as a requirement for her future mate. Ava was overjoyed that Kevin passed that test with flying colors.

They walked to the car hand in hand. As always, he opened the passenger's door then headed to the driver's side. They both wore smiles on their faces. Although they were silent in the car ride over to the church, they still held each other's hands.

Once they arrived at the church, the need for forgiveness wore on Kevin's face. Ava squeezed his hand before exiting the car.

"Thank you, Ava."

"For what?" Ava looked to Kevin.

"For just being the woman I fell in love with. Thank you."

"Kevin, I'm here for you no matter what. I forgive you. Now it's time that you forgive yourself and move forward. Walking through those church doors will be your salvation. Are you ready?"

"Yes. As long as you are by my side, I can get through anything."

Walking through the doors hand in hand, Ava could feel Kevin's heaviness. During worship, Kevin seemed emotional. When the pastor opened the altar up for prayer, he turned to Ava and said, "I want to go up for prayer."

She rubbed his back. "Okay. Do you want me to come with you?"

"I would love for you to." He took hold of her hand and led her to the altar. She felt safe, secure, cared for, and loved.

While the prayer partner spoke over Kevin's situation, he squeezed Ava's hand. The words seemed to saturate themselves into Kevin's soul. God was doing a work in him right then and there.

Proud to be standing there with her man, Ava cherished the moment and promised herself she would remember being at the altar with him for prayer for the rest of her life. *Next time we're up here though, Lord, could we be joining in holy matrimony?* Ava couldn't help herself.

Had things changed for her since she learned he had decided to dabble back into his cocaine habit? She wanted more than anything to believe it was a one-time slip-up, and Ava wouldn't ignore the signs if it wasn't. She did love him, though, and at this point in her life, she believed she could love him through anything. Even drug addiction.

After service, they traveled to Ava's parents' house for an early supper. Kevin caressed her hand as he drove. "Baby, I want to thank you for not running the other way when you heard I fell off the sobriety boat. I appreciate your support and love. It means a lot to me."

"Of course, babe." Ava couldn't contain her huge smile. "And I love you too. I am on your side and want what's best for you. I'm willing to help you get to God's best for you."

"Well, I thank you. You are a treasure and an inspiration to me, and I thank God for you coming into my life."

He was being so sweet. Ava's heart could hardly take it. She looked forward to sharing her business venture news with her family and the new strides in her relationship with Kevin, but most of all, she looked forward to feeling complete around her family. Her parents, brother and his wife, and little niece would all be in attendance. This would be the first time in a long time Ava walked in her parents' home with a real man of God on her arm, someone she was proud to be connected to.

Walking into her parents' house, she burst at the seams with joy. Yet after they had only been there for about a half hour, Kevin asked her dad to go and talk with him privately. He could've been asking for advice in his current situation. He could've been asking for guidance in his life. Whatever the case, Ava wouldn't dare allow herself to go there and think about what she truly hoped he was asking, but she couldn't help herself to think it was finally going to happen. Her dream was finally evolving into reality. She really wanted to eavesdrop as she had done in her childhood days, but she resisted and prayed that if it was to happen, God would make it so.

Chapter Twenty-nine

Kevin sat at his desk at the CCC, trying to muster up enough courage to go and talk to the director. He needed to explain his current situation and deal with the consequences. He wanted to see a friendly face before he divulged his drug use.

Knocking on Glory's door, he sheepishly walked in.

"Hey, Kev. How you doing?" She smiled.

"Not so great right about now." He slumped into the mauve-colored microfiber chair in front of her. "It's been rough for me, to say the least."

She sat up. "What's going on? You and Ava okay?"

"Oh, yeah. We're great. It's nothing like that." Kevin sat straight up. "In fact, she's been a huge help in all that's been going on in my life."

"Well, that's great news. I know she really has a thing for you." Glory chuckled then caught herself. "Oh, and I am so sorry for what happened to Tweet. Sad thing indeed. Greg and I would've been at the funeral, but I went with him to Dallas for a few days for an interview he had."

Kevin's face scrunched into confusion. "You leaving us, girl?"

Shaking her head, she said, "No, just looking with him. Putting a couple of feelers out. If he does get something out of town, he may just take it and commute on the weekends until we get our finances back up to where they need to be."

"I understand." He crossed his legs. Thinking about something else for a change was a welcome break from the embarrassment at hand.

"So, back to the issue at hand. What's going on with you?"

Break over. "Too much." He paused. Would sharing his dirt with Glory really help his situation? He then recalled the scripture about when two or more were gathered in the Lord's name, He was there. She could pray with him before he traipsed into the director's office. "The night of Tweet's funeral, I was, of course, emotional. Feeling guilty, sad, angry, all of the above. And you know that's when the devil does his best work."

"Yep, ain't that the truth."

"One of my patients offered to help me forget about it for a few hours and enjoy a high." Kevin rubbed his face in despair. "And I took him up on it. Before you scold me, which I need and am willing to hear, I can say today that I'm four days clean."

"Ahh, Kev." Glory threw her hands in the air. Shaking her head, she said, "Are you serious? You're playing with me right?"

Lord knows Kevin wanted it to be one big, bad joke, but it wasn't. "I know." He lowered his brow. "And now I need to go and tell the supervisor. I can't keep working here and help others get off drugs when I got back on. The secret would eat me alive. The torment of having that secret would surely lead me back into the lion's den. All my work was erased when I snorted the first line. I could have stopped it, but I didn't. I thought I could handle the temptation and it wouldn't draw me back in. As you have heard, it did. I screwed up. I don't know if I can truly forgive myself for moving backward. Now it's an open sore feeding off my stupidity."

"Well, you don't know how he'll handle it. He knows you were going through a tough time, and the fact that you are willing to come clean and relieve yourself of what you have done will definitely show that you are getting back on the right track."

"Yeah, but as a drug counselor, I'm supposed to use the advice I give my patients. Go to a meeting, call my sponsor. Get busy focusing on something else. Pray. Plus, I wouldn't want to continue working here anyway. At least not until I got another year clean and dealt with my own issues. It just wouldn't be honest with the people I'm helping."

"I understand. Well, God will see you through. Remember that. Do you want to pray before you go talk to him?"

"Of course."

Glory extended her hands. "Dear Lord, we come to you, lifting up my brother, Kevin, and his situation to you. You know his heart and his emotional status, Lord, and you can meet him where he's at and see him through every step of the way. You have been so good to us, Lord, and we know that you wouldn't bring him this far to leave him now."

He squeezed her hands tighter.

She went on, "I pray for his family as they deal with the loss of their loved one. Comfort them every second of the day. And, Lord, right now, please give Kevin the right words to speak as he closes the door here at the CCC. Open a new door of opportunity for him, and let him feel your unconditional love at work in his life. We agree and decree it so. In Jesus' name."

Her words gave him a certain confidence that he carried in with him to the director's office. He knocked on the door lightly.

"Come in."

"Good morning, Director."

"Ahh, good to see you, Kevin. First, let me say I'm so sorry for your loss. I know it can be rough for our loved ones to leave us, but just know she's with God, and He will keep her close to His heart."

"Thank you, Director, but I'm here to resign."

"Kevin, what are you saying? Did something happen? Can I do something for you to reconsider?" The director looked confused by his statement.

Kevin explained everything just as he had to Glory. The director understood his position, prayed for him as well, and let him know he could always come back in a volunteer capacity when he was ready.

Kevin left the director's office with mixed feelings. He had let so many down: his peers, his love, his family. Could he truly recover from this? He walked into his office feeling that this was the last place he wanted to be in his life. One mistake caused him to lose his position at the CCC. He understood why, and he had to move forward and forgive himself for his mistake. If God could, he could too.

Once in his office, he gathered the few possessions he had around the office. Sorrow fell over him. He had spent the last seven years helping those who walked through those doors feeling down and out. Kevin would miss those opportunities, and he vowed to be able to help in that sort of capacity again one day.

As he walked out the doors of the CCC, the sunlight hit his face. A man who looked like he had been through some hard times stared at him.

Kevin, not sure he wanted to bite, did anyway. "May I help you?"

"You probably don't recognize me."

"Can't say that I do."

The man stepped closer. "Well, the last time you saw me, I was under a couple layers of dirt and sitting on the street." He reached in his pocket and pulled out one of Kevin's business cards. "You gave me your card. You gave me hope."

"I do remember you. That was the night I lost my sister."

"Yeah, I know. I did some asking around. I'm sorry for your loss. My name is Chris."

"Well, thank you, Chris. I'm glad you came up here. I'm taking a break from here, but I can point you in the right direction." It felt good to help one last time.

"You are?"

"Yep. I need to handle some personal issues, but I plan to be back one day."

Chris stuck out his hand. "I respect that. Just want you to know that I thought God and everybody else didn't care about me, but you talking to me that night showed me something different. I appreciate it, and if you don't know anything else, know you helped me."

Kevin was on the verge of tears. The two shared a manly hug and parted ways before the first drop of water fell from his eyes. God had placed him in the street that night for more reasons than he knew. Being with his sister and talking with her before she took her last breath would be a moment he would always remember and cherish. He never could help her get fully clean, but in spite of what he currently thought about himself, he had helped someone.

Now, he would need to take some strides to help himself. Seek counseling of his own. Handle his family once and for all, and fully commit to the woman he loved, no matter what his family thought about her or them being together.

He knew exactly where he needed to go and what he needed to do. When he arrived at his car and settled in, Kevin sent a group text to his mother and sisters: Meet at

Mom's house. And come to listen, not talk. Our relationship depends on it.

He waved one more good-bye to the angel the Lord had sent his way at that time, and pulled out of the parking lot. Kevin prayed God would send an extra special blessing Chris's way and lead him down the path of sobriety.

All the way over to his mother's house, Kevin replayed what he would say to them once he laid eyes on their hard faces. By the time he arrived at his mother's home, he was still a bit unclear as to what he was going to say.

As he entered the house and made it to the kitchen table, he believed he knew exactly what he was going to say and how he was going to say it. It would be from his heart solely, saying everything that there was to say about him and Ava without their input or digs.

As he waited for his sisters to arrive, he watched his mother warm up her coffee with a refill. She was excited to have him there and showered him with hugs and kisses when he drifted through the front door, but he had come in and sat down, not speaking. He needed to show his seriousness in the matter.

When all involved parties arrived, he got right to work. He told everyone to gather around the table as he stood. "I love you all more than you will ever know and probably understand." He looked at his mother. "You will always be my momma, and I respect you and take that position you hold in my life very seriously." He turned to Martha and Mary. "And you two have been instrumental in my life, and I love you for that. You've been more than just sisters; you've been my friends."

The three ladies sat looking like they were in the principal's office in elementary school, waiting for their punishment after the lecture.

"But I am a grown man, and my life is just that: my life. I don't tell you all what and what not to do in your lives, so I'd appreciate the same respect. I know you care about me, and that is priceless, but I love Ava, and that's who I want to be with. So your two cents on this matter is not needed or welcome anymore."

His mother grabbed his hand, while his sisters sat quiet. "I know I have a poor way of expressing myself sometimes, but it comes from love. And, Kevin, all I've ever wanted is what's best for you."

He jerked his hand back. "And who's to say Ava isn't my best, Momma?"

"You're right. Only God knows." She hung her head in shame. "But some of the choices she made and how y'all came to meet isn't what I would want for my only son. I want you to be with someone who's honest, true to God, and most of all, one who has no baggage attached to her life."

"Well, people make mistakes, Momma, and they learn from them." He nodded and tapped his fingers on the table. "Not to mention, those mistakes brought her into my life, and I love her with all my heart. I have forgiven her, she's forgiven herself, and, most importantly, God has forgiven her. If you, Martha, and Mary can't forgive her, that's y'all's problem. Not hers. She should not be intimidated by any of you if I bring her around. There will be no more of those hurtful words that come from your mouths."

His mother gasped, along with his sisters.

"I mean it. And I don't know what all our futures have in store for us, but I do know this: I am serious about what I said earlier about losing a son. Your only son." He interlocked his fingers. "And I'll tell you this much: We just lost Tweet, and I'm not about to lose another woman I love because you all can't deal. Do with that what you will." Kevin slapped the table and walked toward the door.

"Where are you going?" Martha held her neck to the side.

"Just gonna give you some time to let everything I just talked about sink in for you." He grabbed his keys. It would be the last time he'd grab anything off that counter if they didn't change. "I'll be available when you're ready to apologize to me and Ava. And maybe then we can finally move on."

By the time he made it to the car, the weight had been lifted off of his shoulders. The ball was in his family's court now. If he needed to, he'd switch the game up altogether. As long as Ava was on his team, all was well.

Chapter Thirty

That following Monday morning, Kevin sat in his comfortable desk chair one last time. He needed a break from looking through the files of his clients to refer them to other counselors. Sitting there quietly, he thought about all the addicts he had helped to get and stay clean. Who could he turn to now and ask for help without being embarrassed? If he had learned anything the first time around, it was that you must get around others who are trying to stay clean and get an accountability partner. Maybe after he left there, he should go to an NA meeting. He obviously needed a refresher course.

He was at a loss for what to do in that moment. The door would probably always be open for him to return in a volunteer capacity, but something in him knew that he wouldn't be back.

Whether it was the irony of it all, being that he was a drug prevention counselor who fell off the drug-free path, or he didn't feel he could help folks stay off drugs anymore since he couldn't help himself, he knew this was his last time to step foot in the building. His heart hurt, as he would miss the coworkers he had been with, most of them for seven years. He would miss being there for struggling addicts.

"Lord, I know that your plan for me is good. Please forgive me for falling to temptation and not asking for your help beforehand." He paused as tears began to roll down his face. "I had just lost Tweet, and I know her addiction was my fault."

Inside his spirit, he heard a resounding voice: *No, it's not. Quit holding on to that burden. I have forgiven you, Tweet has forgiven you, and you need to forgive yourself.*

Kevin stopped in his prayer, opened his eyes, and looked around the room. Could that have been the voice of God? He knew the Lord spoke to people in different ways, but this was the first time that he had ever actually heard a voice speak answers, or anything for that matter.

The main gem he got of those words was forgiveness. Yes, he had introduced Tweet to drugs, but he didn't usher her around the city to find more and harder drugs. He did his best to stop her and guide her to sobriety. Her death could not rest on his shoulders. Choices were made and, as sad as it was, consequences were handed out, but in that moment, he realized that he couldn't live his life with this enormous burden on him. Kevin wouldn't really be living at all if he continued to carry the guilt around with him. His life would suffer, his friends and family would suffer, and most of all, he'd be keeping a part of himself from Ava. That was definitely something he didn't want to do.

He loved her more than anything and wanted to share his life and who he was with her, and that included the good with the bad. He couldn't fully do that if he was holding on to negativity. "Lord, I release myself from this burden and guilt. Please help me to deal with the pain in a healthy way. I love you, Lord, and thank you for loving me unconditionally. In Jesus' name."

The weight had been lifted. Now he could move forward freely. He rose out of the chair and threw his last bit of odds and ends from his desk in a box. Just then his phone buzzed. Hoping it was Ava, he couldn't get to the phone fast enough.

"Hey, bro." It was Martha. A nice surprise, but hearing Ava's voice would've been more therapeutic and timely.

"Hey, sis. How's it going?"

She didn't say much, but the worry in her voice spoke volumes. "Kevin, you need to get to the Healers Hospital ASAP. Momma had a stroke. The doctor said she's stable now, but they are keeping her for observation."

"Oh, no." Yes, he wasn't happy with his family right then, but he'd never wish ill will on any of them, and that was his momma. "Is she awake? Talking?"

"When she did finally wake up, all she asked about was you. Please hurry. Drop whatever you're doing and get over here."

Kevin hit the END button, grabbed the rest of his belongings, and headed out in a hurry. He wanted to stop and thank the director of the CCC one more time, but he didn't have time for that now. He needed to get to his mother. He wouldn't be able to forgive himself this time if he wasn't there for his mother.

Kevin drove like a maniac toward the hospital. He prayed that God would guide his car to his mother's side as fast as He could without him getting pulled over. Thankfully Kevin made it to the hospital in record time. He parked the car and rushed into the hospital. Quickly he called his sister to find out which room their mother was in.

As soon as he walked into Gladys's hospital room, Mary jumped out of her chair. "Kevin, so good to see you."

"Good to see you too." Giving her a hug as he watched his mother sleeping, he said, "How's Momma doing?"

"She's much better now." Martha walked over by her mother's side. "And I know when she wakes she'll want to talk with you." Grabbing her purse, she turned to Mary. "Why don't we let Kev be alone with Momma? It'll be a nice surprise for her to wake up and see him here."

Mary shrugged her shoulders. "Cool."

As Kevin sat next to his mother in the most uncomfortable vinyl chair, he adored her. She

was resting and at peace, seemingly pain free for the moment. They had a few difficult past weeks and days, but they were family. Whatever was going on between them, they could talk about it and move on. He loved his mother and he loved Ava. And that love would guide their relationships and working through their issues.

Kevin sent Ava a quick text that read: Visiting Mom in the hospital. She had a stroke but she is okay now. I'll give you the details when I see you tonight. Love you!

With Tweet gone and his mother in the hospital, Kevin knew he wanted to go forward

with the plans for his life and the possibilities that could be found as he and Ava continued to keep God first in their relationship. He wouldn't listen to his mother, his sisters, or even to his own doubts of himself. He had never felt this way about a woman he had been in a relationship with. Kevin knew he'd found the one. His soul mate. And he could only hope she felt the same way.

Chapter Thirty-one

Two months had passed since Ava signed the loan papers, and she couldn't believe she was standing in the middle of her new restaurant, Manna Blessings Café. The location was perfect, with her lawyer best friend's office right next door. Folks would have to think twice before taking a slip and fall or trying to sue her for some unnecessary reason.

Her modern, chic décor worked together with the grand opening decorations, as people filled every corner of the restaurant. All of her family was there, her girlfriends and spouses, and even Kevin's family made it to the event.

It almost seemed like Kevin's mother lurked around until she saw Ava was alone. "Congratulations, Ava." She opened her arms for a hug and even had a smile on her face.

Ava, not sure she wanted to fall for any fakeness, still wanted to be the bigger person and reciprocated the embrace. She held her breath for any snide remarks. "Thank you, Gladys. I appreciate you all being here."

"Where else would we be? Kevin is important to us, and you are important to him."

Ava smiled. Finally, Gladys had come to realize that fact. Ava wasn't going anywhere as long as Kevin wanted to keep her around. There was no doubt about that.

She motioned for her daughters to come over to her as she took hold of Ava's hand. "I just want to apologize for how we've treated you, Ava. We have always been protective of our Kevin, but that's no excuse to be nasty to you. We were being childish, and Kevin helped us to see that."

"Well, thank you." Relaxing her guard just a bit, Ava grinned. *Finally they all see the light.*

"I mean it. Please don't hold our ignorance against us. We are really a loving group of women. I know we haven't shown it, but we are, and we can be fun, too." She smiled. "And we all look forward to spending more time with you so we can truly get to know one another. Will you accept our apology and forgive us?"

"Of course I will. Like you said, you all are important to Kevin, and he is important to me, so I want us to get along to ease his stress. Who knows? We may end up being close as well. You know, I can be loving and even fun, too, so I look forward to starting over with you ladies on a good solid foot. No more reliving our past mistakes. We all love Kevin and want to see him happy."

Ava embraced his sisters, and for the first time felt truly accepted by his family. She would remember that feeling, and she hoped it would grow as the days went on.

As she scanned the room, she reflected on how the Lord had done His thing again. He orchestrated the mending of her relationship with Kevin's family and brought the two of them closer together.

Glory and Greg were all smiles and loving toward one another. Eric was busy rubbing Toni's pregnant belly as he made silly noises and talked to it in his best baby talk voice. Rene and Paul were oblivious to everyone else in the room as they acted like the newlyweds they were. Ava made mental notes of the lessons learned from each of her three friends' relationships that she could take into her own relationship.

Glory taught her how she could use what she was going through to help someone else one day. Speaking from personal experience offered others a firsthand account of what God could do in their life if they'd put Him first. The situation, no matter how difficult, could allow others to see and believe their situation could turn around too.

Rene had shown Ava how to close the door on the past, so she could enjoy all that God had in store for her future. The Lord didn't stay in the past, so why should she? Her past relationships were a true hot mess, but now she was involved with a man of God, who treated her as the gem that she was created to be. He had his flaws, like everyone else, but she could deal with whatever came about between them, because she loved him. They'd already made it through a breakup, death of a loved one, and a drug relapse, but he was the real deal, and she cherished what they had together. The other men in her past were just steps along the way to get her to Kevin.

Toni's lesson would probably prove to be the most beneficial of them all. Ava learned from Toni to keep her trust in God and not in the man. Only God could change in him what needed to be changed and direct his steps. All she had to do was love him, pray for him, and support him in every way possible. Her trust would remain in the Lord, as He facilitated the ins and outs of their relationship. She wholeheartedly put her faith in God and would allow Him to do His best work in their relationship. She'd just sit back and enjoy the ride.

Kevin's clinking of his fork on his glass broke her thoughts but got everyone's attention. "I just wanted to take this time to congratulate my beautiful girlfriend and her dream of being a restaurateur coming true. I hope she'll give me a job, since I am looking." He laughed. "No, but for real, she deserves for all of her dreams to come true." He grabbed her hand and pulled her to the center of the room. He watched her eyes move side to side like a kid on Christmas morning, deciding which gift to open first.

Pulling a small box out of his jacket pocket, he got down on one knee. Gasps filled the room. Ava stood speechless, taking in the moment she had waited for all her life. This was finally it. She would have everything she wanted by the grace of God.

"You have been what I have been waiting for God to give me in a wife. I love you and want to spend the rest of my life with you. I want the honor of making you happy for the rest of your life. So I have to ask: Ava Alexander, will you marry me?"

Everything around Ava stopped as she gazed into Kevin's eyes. A silent tear rolled down her soft cheek and rested on her chin. "Kevin, you are my evidence of things not seen, the substance of my faith, and I love you with all my heart. Of course I will marry you. Yes! Yes! Yes!"

Cheers filled the room as Kevin gently placed the cushion-cut amethyst and diamond ring in a fourteen-karat white gold setting on her finger. He then jumped to his feet and picked up his future wife, planting a simple show of affection on her lips. It was sealed with a kiss. Their lives were now beginning without any past doubts, resentment, or shame.

Ava's elation spilled out all over the restaurant. God knew all along how and when He wanted her dreams to play out. All she had to do was have faith and believe, and wait for His perfect timing. The restaurant, her fiancé—yep, the Lord had answered her prayers, and He did it in a very convincing fashion, like only He could.

Ava's joy touched everyone in the room. Her girls gathered around her, hugging and kissing her, for she was finally going to be at the altar. Her mother squeezed in and hugged her daughter. There were no words, just tears of joy for both of them. They both felt their dreams had come true. God had worked on Ava's heart, mind, body, and soul to restore her self-esteem, and most of all, her forgiveness to herself. She struggled with it all, and God led her through the thorn-filled bushes without injury. Now all her blessings were waiting.

Ava relished the surprise of Kevin's proposal. She already had everything planned out on paper and in her mind, but she didn't want to rush anything. For once, she would slow things down and enjoy her blessings from God.

Kevin's family pulled him out of Ava's circle. He didn't know if they were happy for them or reverting to their old ways. He hoped for the better. His mother was the first to speak.

"Kevin, is this what you truly want?"

"Yes, Momma."

She smiled at him and hugged him tightly. "I am happy for the both of you. I'm happy that you are happy. I love you and will learn to love Ava too."

"Thank you, Momma. That's all I wanted."

"Okay, okay, enough of the mushy stuff. I have cried enough. Kevin, I'm happy that you found the love of your life, and I just want to say I'm sorry for never seeing all that you truly do for us. I will be a better sister to you. I promise. I only hope you can forgive us for putting so much onto you." Martha kissed him on the cheek and hugged him tightly.

"Me too," Mary added.

"Is that all you have to say, Mary?" Martha twisted her lips.

"Yeah, you guys said it all. No need to say it a third time."

Kevin smiled and hugged his family. "I love you all."

"Hey, can I get in on this?" Ava smiled with open arms.

"Of course you can." Gladys grabbed her by the hip for a tight squeeze.

"This is absolutely one of the best nights of my life," Ava said.

"One of the best nights?" Kevin questioned.

"Yes. The best night of my life will be our wedding night, of course."

They all laughed in unison.

"Come on, y'all. Let's celebrate, for we have the entire night to relish this joy." Ava pulled Kevin to dance and enjoy the celebration.

Ava and Kevin stood in the middle of the room with their heads bowed. They both gave thanks to the Lord for all He had done in His timing.

Readers' Discussion Questions

1. Did Ava handle all her situations in a godly manner? Were there times she felt the need to react on impulse? Would you act in this manner?
2. Did you think Rene was right to ask Ava to accompany her to see Ishmael? If not, why?
3. Should Kevin have stopped his mother and sisters sooner for acting in such a rude manner? Was it right for him to take a break?
4. Did Ava act as a doormat when Kevin had to leave her side unexpectedly to attend to his family's issues? Would you allow it to happen again?
5. Do you think Kevin was right to reveal Ava's past to his mother? What would you do in that situation?
6. Did Ava act in the appropriate manner when she gave Kevin an ultimatum? Was she too harsh?
7. When Kevin revealed his mistake of falling off the wagon, should Ava have taken him back? If not, why?
8. Would you have kept his mistake a secret and worked through it on your own? Why did he feel the need to leave the place where he had helped so many after just one slip-up?
9. Ava gave in to the enemy in Jamaica. Would you do the same? Why do you think Ava withheld that truth from Kevin? Was she that scared of losing him all over again?

10. When Kevin's mother had a stroke, was it God's will to bring the family back together?
11. Did you think Ava had her own addiction to deal with? Why didn't her friends see her addiction?
12. Do you think Kevin's family was sincere enough to Ava after Kevin proposed?
13. Will Ava ever get over her past, or will it show its ugly face again?

UC HIS GLORY BOOK CLUB!

www.uchisglorybookclub.net

UC His Glory Book Club is the spirit-inspired brain-child of Joylynn Ross, Author and Acquisitions Editor of Urban Christian, and Kendra Norman-Bellamy, Author for Urban Christian. This is an online book club that hosts authors of Urban Christian. We welcome as members all men and women who have a passion for reading Christian-based fiction.

UC His Glory Book Club pledges our commitment to provide support, positive feedback, encouragement, and a forum whereby members can openly discuss and review the literary works of Urban Christian authors.

There is no membership fee associated with UC His Glory Book Club; however, we do ask that you support the authors through purchasing, encouraging, providing book reviews, and of course, your prayers. We also ask that you respect our beliefs and follow the guidelines of the book club. We hope to receive your valuable input, opinions, and reviews that build up, rather than tear down our authors.

What We Believe:

—We believe that Jesus is the Christ, Son of the Living God.

—We believe the Bible is the true, living Word of God.

—We believe all Urban Christian authors should use their God-given writing abilities to honor God and share the message of the written word God has given to each of them uniquely.

—We believe in supporting Urban Christian authors in their literary endeavors by reading, purchasing, and sharing their titles with our online community.

—We believe that everything we do in our literary arena should be done in a manner that will lead to God being glorified and honored.

We look forward to the online fellowship with you.

Please visit us often at:

www.uchisglorybookclub.net.

Many Blessings to You!

Shelia E. Lipsey,
President, UC His Glory Book Club